W9-BDF-727

Phyllis and Addie sat cross-legged on pillows, facing each other, knees touching. Gwyneth sat with her back to the fire, a notebook and pencil poised to take down what the Ouija said. They bent over the board like three small witches concentrating on a spell, while outside the rain crashed down, sometimes straight down and sometimes almost horizontal, blown by the wind.

So intent were they on the board that they did not hear the front door open. Had they looked up, through the open door between the drawing room and the entry hall, they would have seen a dark overcoated figure step into the hall. But they did not look up.

The figure started toward the stairs. He did not at first take the trouble to be quiet, but his footsteps blended with the sounds of the storm outside. The figure stopped short, however, at the foot of the stairs, his eye attracted to the drawing room door, to a flickering circle of firelight beyond it, to the three small silhouettes clustered around the circle of fire. The figure stopped, and watched the scene. It was some moments before the figure turned and continued up the stairs.

"Was Lucie Jackson murdered?" asked Addie in a voice that made Phyllis shiver.

The Ouija Board Murder

by Judith Vannice

tempo
books

GROSSET & DUNLAP
A FILMWAYS COMPANY
Publishers • New York

THE OUIJA BOARD MURDER
Copyright © 1978 by Judith Vannice
All Rights Reserved
Published simultaneously in Canada
ISBN: 0-448-14765-3
Tempo Books is registered in the U.S. Patent Office
A Tempo Books Original
Printed in the United States of America

Chapter One

"Don't be morbid, Addie," said Gwyneth.

"All I'm saying is, I think he killed her. That's all I'm saying."

"I don't think Mr. Linn would do a thing like that," said Phyllis.

It was Tuesday, New Year's night. The year had not come in very willingly, it seemed, and for the second night in a row rain poured down. Last night's storm had worsened, however, and tonight's was a regular gale.

The big Pennsylvania house which was Mrs. Otto's Boarding School for Girls was having trouble heating itself. Generally, despite the building's age and its high ceilings, the physical and psychological warmth generated by its twenty-one female students was enough to keep things comfortable. But tonight was still technically vacation. Classes would not start for three more days, and only Gwyneth, Addie and Phyllis had returned thus far; Gwyneth and Addie returned this morning. Phyllis' mother had deposited Phyllis at the school two days earlier and had taken herself off to Majorca to recuperate from all the Christmas festivities.

Armed with pillows stolen from the sofa and mugs of hot chocolate, the three girls were gathered around the drawing room fireplace, their backs to the windows against which the rain beat. The room was dark except for the firelight.

They were alone in the room, a rare treat. Generally there was someone hovering ("always hovering," said Addie), watching over them. But most of the watchers—with the exception of Mrs. Otto—were on holiday.

Mrs. Otto, much against her will, had retired to her bedroom with the beginnings of a bad case of post-holiday flu.

Only two of the servants were still there. Alex Campbell the gardener had his own small house in back (more of a shed than a house), where he spent his evenings. The cook was gone for the holiday, leaving only Sarah Bow the maid to occupy the basement servants' quarters. Sarah had retired, after having been cajoled into making hot chocolate for the girls.

All but three of the instructors had gone to visit family or friends for the holiday. Mrs. Beatrice Withers, having no family, had remained at the school and was presently upstairs in her room reading. Mr. Paul Linn, having no family he could tolerate for much more than five minutes at a time, had also stayed at the school but wasn't around at the moment. Miss Lucie Jackson, teacher of drama and dance, had died in her bed the night before.

"Murdered," Addie was saying. "Suffocated with a pillow, most likely."

"She was *not*," said Gwyneth. "Mrs. Otto said she died of natural causes. She had a weak heart."

"That's what Mrs. Otto told *us*. But that's not what happened. She was trying to spare our delicate feelings. Not to mention sparing herself a nasty scandal. Murdered," Addie repeated. "I heard the gardener and Sarah talking."

"That's just gossip. They're just servants," scorned Gwyneth. Gwyneth distrusted Addie. She knew for sure she was a liar and suspected her to be a thief as well. Still . . . a murder. Not just a simple died-in-one's-bed, but *killed*-in-one's-bed. A murder! A thrill went all the way to Gwyneth's toes.

"Just what exactly, specifically, did they say?" she asked.

"It was Alex mostly. Saying how strange it was that the police stayed around so much last night. Saying how some of those questions they asked seemed awfully strange to him."

"Well, if it was murder, how come your uncle didn't come then?" demanded Gwyneth. "I thought he was supposed to be in charge of all the murder cases or something like that."

"He is," said Addie, "but I think he was out of town. My mother said something about him spending Christmas with my grandparents. He ought to be back by today, though. I wish he *had* been here last night. He'd have known it was murder."

She turned to Phyllis. "I wish you'd been awake and seen something, Phyllis. How could you have slept through a murder?"

"Well, everybody else did," Phyllis pointed out defensively. "Besides, I never thought for a minute it *was* murder. They woke me up, they asked me if I'd heard anything but I hadn't, and I was scared, and Mrs. Otto said not to upset me, and they let me go back to bed."

"But you were on the very same floor—just right down the hall. I bet if I'd been here, I'd have seen something."

Phyllis pouted.

"Well, anyway," Addie continued, "It's murder,' Alex said. 'You mark my words.' And Sarah Bow went all hysterical the way she does and said, 'Murdered. Oh my. But who'd murder Miss Lucie?' And on and on. And Alex said, 'You'd better be careful in your bed at night, Sarah—could be the murderer's all set to pounce on you next,' being terribly funny, you know. And she sort of giggled, but she looked really scared. And then of course the idiot had to pretend to be a murderer and tiptoe up behind her and grab her . . . anyway, *that* part is unimportant," said Addie. "The point is, Miss Jackson was murdered."

"So that's why Sarah's been acting so funny,"

mused Phyllis. "I walked into the kitchen this afternoon and she shrieked and dropped the butter dish and the butter all over the floor. I thought that was strange."

"Well, I don't know," said Gwyneth. "There's no evidence."

"I don't care whether you believe me or not. All I'm saying is, it's true. She was murdered. And Paul Linn is my choice for murderer. I feel it."

"I know what," said Phyllis. "Let's ask the Ouija board. It'll tell us if she was really murdered, *and* it'll tell us who did it."

"Well," said Gwyneth, "it won't prove anything."

"Please," said Phyllis.

"I guess it would be evidence," said Gwyneth, "It wouldn't prove anything, but it would be evidence. All right. I'll go up and get the board."

The Ouija board was forbidden by Mrs. Otto as being "nonsense". "If you have nothing better to do with your time," she would say, "perhaps the workload here is too light. I will speak to the instructors." So the Ouija board was hidden under Gwyneth's bed, along with the poker chips and certain assorted movie magazines. Gwyneth was guardian of all their vices.

"Do you really think Mr. Linn did it?" whispered Phyllis after Gwyneth had gone. She pulled at a lock of dark hair, tugging until the curl had nearly gone out of it.

"Of course. She was in love with him—there

were indications. He probably led her on and then tired of her. Maybe he even met someone else. But she had some sort of hold on him, too. . ."

"You mean like blackmail?"

"Not necessarily money blackmail. Just some reason why he couldn't leave her, and he wanted to. I wonder what that reason was. . ."

Addie looked into the fire. Phyllis started to follow her gaze, then hesitated. Sometimes the girls played a game of looking for castles and dragons and bridges in the firelight. Phyllis was afraid to look into the fire now. Supposing she saw Miss Jackson's face there? Miss Jackson, who was now dead.

"Here's the Ouija," announced Gwyneth.

Phyllis jumped. Even Addie was momentarily startled out of her concentration.

"That was quick," she said. "I didn't even hear you. Well, let's get started, shall we?"

Gwneth looked at Addie suspiciously. "All right, but I think Phyllis and I should work the board and you should watch. How do we know you won't just make it say what you want it to say?"

"I never do that. Besides," said Addie smugly, "you know it never works for you. You're a skep-tic."

"I am not." But it was true. Every time Gwyneth sat behind the Ouija board, no matter how tightly she shut her eyes and how hard she concentrated, the little heart-shaped marker sat stubbornly still—no matter who her partner was. "Oh, all right," she said crossly.

Phyllis and Addie sat cross-legged on pillows, facing each other, knees touching. Gwyneth sat with her back to the fire, a notebook and pencil poised to take down what the Ouija said. They bent over the board like three small witches concentrating on a spell, while outside the rain poured down and was blown furiously around by the wind.

So intent were they on the board that they did not hear the front door open. Had they looked up, through the open door between the drawing room and the entry hall, they would have seen a dark overcoated figure step into the hall. But they didn't look up.

The figure started toward the stairs. He did not at first take the trouble to be quiet, but his footsteps blended with the sounds of the storm outside. The figure stopped short, however, at the foot of the stairs, his eye attracted to the drawing room door, to a flickering circle of firelight beyond it, to the three small silhouettes clustered around the circle of fire. The figure stopped, and watched the scene. It was some time before the figure turned and continued up the stairs.

"Was Lucie Jackson murdered?" asked Addie in a voice that made Phyllis shiver. Addie could make the Ouija seem not a game at all. She forced herself to close her eyes against Addie's secret, absorbed expression and tried herself to concentrate on the fatal question: "Was Lucie Jackson murdered?"

The Ouija was moving. Phyllis knew it was a rule not to open her eyes, but she didn't need to. She could feel the marker under her hands moving steadily toward the "yes" side of the board. It stopped. "Yes," breathed Gwyneth.

Upstairs, Mrs. Otto was restless. It had been a mistake to go to bed so early. She hadn't been sleeping well lately, and having the flu didn't help matters. She always despised insomniacs and their endless complaints. She needed a long quiet night of sleep.

Upstairs, too, the house almost perceptibly shook with the fury of the storm outside. The storm's noise contrasted oddly with the silence inside, the silence of a house used to having people in it, a house not accustomed to being so deserted.

A particularly vicious gust of wind blew, slapping rain hard against Mrs. Otto's window. Mrs. Otto sighed, and knew it was going to be a long time before sleep would come tonight. She had learned to recognize the signs. She put back the covers and slipped on her wrapper, then stood in indecision. What to do now? A book, a cup of milk? All the things that were supposed to work, and didn't.

Addie had taken her hands away from the board momentarily to brush her hair from her face. With renewed concentration, she returned to the board. "Who murdered Lucie Jackson?"

The Ouija hesitated, then spelled out: P-O-L L-I-N.

Phyllis gasped.

"It never could spell very well," said Addie.

"You're not supposed to *look*," hissed Gwyneth. "I'm the only one who's supposed to look."

"All right." Addie shut her eyes obediently and asked one word: "How?"

The Ouija hesitated.

"Probably can't spell 'suffocate'," said Addie. "We'll make it easy: Did she suffocate?"

The Ouija hesitated again, then spelled out quickly: P-A-U-L L-I-N.

"We know that, stupid," snapped Gwyneth. "But how?"

"Don't provoke it," said Addie. "At least its spelling has improved. Let's ask it something else. Was Miss Jackson in love with Mr. Linn?"

Yes, the Ouija spelled out.

"Was he having an affair with her?" Addie went on.

"Was she blackmailing him?" Phyllis asked excitedly before she could stop herself.

Gwyneth gave her a surprised look, Addie a withering one.

Yes, said the Ouija.

"You dope. Now we don't know which question it's answering. We'll have to ask it all over again."

A tiny rustling sound from behind her registered in Addie's mind, a split second too late. They were no longer alone in the room.

"Ask what all over again?" came a frosty voice from the doorway.

"Mrs. Otto!" whispered Phyllis.

"Mrs. Otto," sighed Addie.

The sight of Mrs. Otto angry, even weak and feverish as she was, was enough to intimidate anyone. And Mrs. Otto was very, very angry. She stood in the doorway, the light from the fire catching her dark green robe and turning it an eerie, glowing color. ("Like the witch in Sleeping Beauty," Gwyneth whispered later.) Her face was nearly all in shadow; the light from the fire did not reach that high. And somehow, not being able to see her eyes made it all even more frightening.

"You will all go to your rooms," she said in a quiet, deadly voice.

Gwyneth began to gather up the Ouija board and marker.

"No," said Mrs. Otto. "I'll take that. You are never to touch that again."

Addie, Gwyneth and Phyllis stole past her, not daring to look up. They slunk up the stairs, afraid of every creak their feet made on the stairs, afraid of arousing that quiet anger again.

Just as she reached the top of the circular staircase, Addie turned around to take one last look back down—and what she saw made her pause another moment longer.

She saw Lenore Otto lean wearily against the doorjamb, staying there several moments before crossing over to the fire to pick up the sofa pillows. She returned them to their proper places.

Mrs. Otto began, too, to gather up the empty mugs to take to the kitchen. But she paused in this, and looked into the fire. At last Addie could see her face.

Though Lenore Otto was a handsome woman, the firelight played unflattering tricks on her this night. It deepened the hollows of her cheekbones and eyes, and cast a red and unnatural glow onto her face.

She put a hand to her lips, and spoke aloud. Addie was sure she heard the words correctly.

"What am I going to do now?" said Mrs. Otto. "What now?"

Safe in their room, Addie and Phyllis sat cross-legged on Phyllis' patchwork quilt. Gwyneth sat at the mirror brushing her hair. Phyllis, her head bent over the quilt, traced with her finger one plump shepherdess among the many plump shepherdesses sewn in patchwork. Addie stared out the window.

"What I think," she said at length, "is there's something strange about all this. Something really, really strange."

Gwyneth and Phyllis looked at her.

"Well, there is," she insisted. "Have you ever seen Mrs. Otto angry before—I mean really, truly angry like she was tonight? She's found us out with the Ouija board before, and she's never behaved like this."

"Maybe she's just upset about Miss Jackson," Phyllis ventured. "And worried for the school—you know, that our parents might not want us to stay here now there's been a murder."

"If it was murder," Gwyneth put in. "Don't forget that."

"Still," said Addie. "I think we should watch. For clues. It's odd. Just . . . odd. I have a feeling. I don't think the Ouija has told us everything."

Her eyes met Gwyneth's in the mirror. Gwyneth shivered.

Chapter Two

Paul Linn stepped into his room, shut the door behind him, and unbuttoned his overcoat. He was cheerful before he entered the house, but what he had just witnessed made him furious, and the strain of keeping the fury inside was written in the expression on his face. For a moment he stood before the mirror above his bed, then turned away. He took off his overcoat, shook the rain off, and dropped it in a heap on the bed.

"Snoops!" he said aloud through clenched teeth. "Lying, sneaking, prying little devils, little creatures. What am I doing in this damned place anyway? Doesn't anybody around here mind his own business?" Paul took off a rain-soaked hat and threw it irritably in the approximate direction of the overcoat.

He crossed over to the cupboard and took out a bottle of brandy, the last of his Christmas cache. He got out a glass too—not a proper snifter, but it would do—and poured his first shot. This he disposed of efficiently, and poured another. And another. That was much better. He leaned back precariously in his chair and stretched his legs out on the table.

People who thought they knew Paul Linn were often surprised at the way his cheerful good nature could erupt into waves of violent anger in a moment, and then subside again as if he had never been angry. Paul leaned back further in his chair, his fury of a moment ago seemingly forgotten.

"Hey ho," sang Paul, "the wind and the rain!" He held the glass up to the light and squinted. Somebody had once told him that he could judge the quality of a brandy by its clarity. Paul examined the glass closely, first from one angle, then from another. "Can't tell," he concluded cheerfully. "For the rain it raineth every day," he caroled. "Hey ho! Cheers, Mrs. Otto, you old bat, wherever you are in this mausoleum."

There was a knock at the door.

"Uh oh," whispered Paul to the brandy bottle. He put a finger to his lips. Gently he picked up the bottle and glass and returned them to the cupboard. "You stay there," he said. "I'll be right back."

"Oh, Mr. Linn. I do hope I'm not disturbing you." Beatrice Withers smiled brilliantly as she stepped into his room (and it was a brilliant smile indeed, her lips having been coated liberally with new "Crimson Caress" she had bought herself for Christmas.) Though she received no answer, she went on, undaunted. "I was in my room trying to read and I just couldn't help hearing you come in. Why, I said to myself, it's just not like Mr. Linn to be such an early bird. He's usually out till all hours of the night, I said. Take last night—why, I never did hear you come in." Paul frowned, and Beatrice Withers hurried on. "So, not being nosey, you understand, but I was concerned. I *thought* you looked peaked at dinner, and what with all that flu going on. . . . So I thought, well, I'll just brew some of my special peppermint tea and see if poor Mr. Linn wants to come and have some. It has wonderful calmative powers." She looked at him expectantly.

"I see," said Paul. "Well, thank you very much, Beatrice, but I have my own specially-brewed, er, tea, and it has wonderful calmative powers of its own." Paul Linn politely tried to steer Mrs. Withers in the direction of the door, but without success.

"Oh?" she said, looking about. "Oh?" She maneuvered her way over to the window, and sat down in Paul's chair. "The fact is, Mr. Linn, I've been so distressed. Just so distressed over all this horrid business, haven't you? I just felt that I needed someone to talk to, someone to calm me. This is all so upsetting." Paul waited, fidgeting.

She went on. "*So* upsetting. No one saying anything, no one admitting anything. But I'm sure, aren't you? Lucie Jackson was murdered, as sure as I am sitting here." She tapped the side of the chair for emphasis.

"Don't think about it," said Paul comfortingly. "Why don't you just go back to your room, have some of your, uh, peppermint tea and go straight off to sleep. Things will look brighter in the morning." He looked longingly at the side cupboard.

"The thing is," Mrs. Withers continued, "she was so obviously murdered. Don't you think? I mean people, perfectly healthy people, don't just come home from New Year's Eve parties, get into bed, and 'whoosh', just simply die. They just don't do that. Don't you agree, Mr. Linn?"

"Well no, Beatrice, as a matter of fact I don't. Stranger things than that happen. Besides, Mrs. Otto said she had some sort of heart trouble, rheumatic fever when she was a child, something like that. So you see. . ."

Mrs. Withers got up from the table. Paul moved quickly to the door to usher her out. But Beatrice was not going toward the door. She walked over to Paul's dressing table, took a quick look in the mirror, patted her hair, and peered around. She seemed to be looking for something.

"She was very pretty, though, don't you think? Did you think she was pretty? Of course, I myself have never cared for that type—red hair and light skin seems to give a rather washed-out look. I myself think brown hair is more attractive. Do you agree, Mr. Linn?" Beatrice Withers had brown hair.

Mr. Linn did not say whether he agreed or not.

"You have no photographs around, Mr. Linn. No little personal mementos at all, have you ever thought about that? You're a mystery man, Mr. Linn," she teased. "No one would know anything about you, from looking at this room. But I suppose that men living by themselves are that way. Don't have time for all those little personal touches that women think of. It's those little personal touches that make a room seem homey, though. Do you know, Mr. Linn, that this is the first time I've ever been in your room?"

"Yes," said Paul. "Oh, yes."

"In my room, for instance, I have just all kinds of photographs and little things pinned up. Most women do." Beatrice finished her tour of the room and returned to the table, where she sat down. Paul Linn sighed.

"Yes, this is all terribly upsetting. I realize I'm rambling—I do apologize—I always do this when I get upset. It's a trait of high-strung people to chatter on when they become upset. And I am very highly strung. I do hope you don't mind, Mr. Linn."

Paul made an uninterpretable sound.

"I suppose things won't be nearly the same without Lucie around. The students will be terribly upset. Of course I must admit," Beatrice said, "that I was not terribly fond of her. She seemed quite shallow to me. But one mustn't speak ill of the dead. And of course, I assume *you* were quite fond of her."

"I?" Paul asked, startled. For once he gave Beatrice his full attention.

"Why, yes. Or at least, I know she was fond of you. I notice things," she said in a soft voice, "more than anyone realizes."

"Why, if it had been you that had died, I'm sure Lucie would have been just devastated." Beatrice looked closely at Paul Linn.

Paul's voice took on an odd tone. "Mrs. Withers. I assure you Miss Jackson and I were not in the slightest bit close. You are mistaken. And if we had been, you would not have known it. I am not one to show my feelings. I keep my emotions, grief, fear, an-noy-ance . . . to myself. You must not try to read me, Beatrice. I am not a book."

He smiled slightly, and Beatrice Withers giggled with uncertainty. It was so difficult to know, sometimes, whether Paul Linn was joking or whether he wasn't.

"And now," he continued, "much as I would like to continue this delightful conversation, I'm afraid that your observations about me earlier were correct. I am peaked. I do have a headache. I should like to go straight to bed." This time he propelled her, not quite politely, to the door.

"Oh, Mr. Linn. I do apologize. Honestly, running on like this, I'm so ashamed. I do this every time I get upset—it's just a trait I have." She put her hand on the doorknob, then turned back once more. "And if your cup of tea doesn't do the trick, you come right on over and get some

of mine. I've found it does wonders for head-aches. My door is always open ... to you."
Beatrice blushed, and opened the door.

Mrs. Otto stood there. Her hand was raised, poised to knock. "Oh dear," said Beatrice, blushing brighter. Mrs. Otto would not approve of her visiting a man's room. "Oh dear," she said again.

But Mrs. Otto did not at the moment seem concerned about Beatrice Withers' morals. "I'm glad I found you both in," she said. "I've just had a phone call from the police. They've found marks on Lucie's neck. Very faint marks—they think they were made by a bathrobe cord or a sheet—but they're sure she's been strangled. They're coming in the morning to investigate. They want to question everyone."

Chapter Three

Police Inspector Harrison Emery awoke the next morning after a restless sleep. It was his first night home after a hectic Christmas vacation, and he had been looking forward to a relaxing rest. The news of the murder had greeted him as soon as he returned, and had weighed on his mind all night.

The whole thing seemed somehow his fault. There simply weren't that many violent crimes committed in Delenbridge. He felt vaguely guilty that he had let one occur while he was out of town.

Not being immediately at the scene of the crime had set him back one step already. His absence was more frustrating still when Harrison though of all his recent efforts to prove himself on the Delenbridge police force. Though he was no longer the youngest man on the force, and though he recently had been promoted, he was still referred to as "that young guy." Harrison sighed. He'd probably be "the young guy" on the force until he was forty-five—Delenbridge was like that.

It didn't help, he thought, that he looked younger than his thirty years. There was something about his craggy features and unruly hair, and most of all his slightly buck teeth, that made him look like somebody's older brother, away at college.

Harrison looked at himself in the bedroom mirror and grimaced. . .

The smell of fresh coffee wafted up from downstairs, stirring him from his thoughts. After waiting restlessly all night for morning to come, here he was daydreaming! He jumped out of bed and headed for the bathroom. In a few minutes he was on his way downstairs, following the coffee aroma.

Harrison rented one half of a large, somewhat ramshackle farmhouse owned by a Delenbridge oldtimer named Matthew Gregory. The two men kept their "halves" inviolably separate, with the exception of the kitchen. Since Matthew considered himself a cook and Harrison did not, the sharing of the kitchen posed no problems. Matthew, a confirmed and crusty bachelor, would never consider renting to anyone who had ideas of interfering with his kitchen. Harrison had no such ideas.

Matt was at the stove, scrambling eggs, when Harrison walked into the kitchen. "Been listenin' to the news," he said in his habitual mournful tone, looking up briefly as Harrison went to the coffeepot and poured a cup. "Guess you've got your work cut out."

"Yeah. The murder." Harrison, in Matt's company, often found himself falling into the same clipped speech patterns. He was going to turn into a crusty old bachelor himself if he didn't watch out, he reflected. Matthew's rule of thumb was never to use two words if one would do—and no words at all were better still.

"What'd you hear about it?" he asked the older man.

" 'Police confirmed last night that death of teacher Lucinda Jackson at Mrs. Otto's School was murder. Body was found the morning of January first . . .' etc. Not much more. What's up, anyway? How come it needed 'confirming'? Didn't they know right off it was murder?"

"No. She was strangled, and it was done with a soft material, like a sheet or bathrobe cord, which left only the faintest marks. You wouldn't notice them unless you were looking for them. I wish I'd been there. Willes handled it, and he's pretty new." Harrison took a large gulp of coffee. Matthew must make the strongest coffee in the county, he reflected, but this morning it was just what he needed. "Also," he continued, "the examining doctor said he was told the woman had a weak heart. Heart failure can look like a lot of things. He didn't question it at first, just jumped to that conclusion. It was a reasonable one under the circumstances, I guess. . . Well, it can't be helped now."

"Got any suspects yet?" Matthew set down the plate of eggs and joined Harrison at the table.

"No, not yet. I talked to Willes last night just briefly, but it's too early to tell anything yet. I'll have to go out there myself right away."

"Don't you have a niece who goes to school there? That little girl—Adelaide, isn't it? Funny name for a kid. She was here once with her mother visiting you, I remember. 'Bout a year ago. Couldn't say much for the mother, even if she is your sister. But that was a funny little kid. Not a bad little kid." This was high praise from Matthew Gregory.

Harrison choked on his coffee. "Not a bad little kid! Are you crazy? She's a terror! She is the primary reason why I have decided never to have children. Have you forgotten what happened on that visit? Sally rattled on the whole time about her divorce and talked me out of three hundred dollars—and Addie shaved the fur off the cat with my razor when no one was looking. Have you forgotten that?"

"Just high spirits, that's all," said Matt placidly. "Besides, that was more than a year ago. She was only, what, twelve then, wasn't she? Bright little kid. Say, aren't you kinda worried about her out there, with a murder and all?"

Harrison put down his coffee cup and slapped a hand to his forehead. "Oh lord, I hadn't thought of that. If Sally gets wind of this, she'll be calling here every five minutes or—good lord, worse than that—flying down. And of course she'll blame me for the entire affair. Listen, Matt, if my sister calls, you don't know where I am. You have no idea how to reach me."

"Okay. That's fine with me. I don't want that woman here again. Once was enough."

Harrison picked up his cup again, then paused. He stared into the cup. "She may not even find out right away," he consoled himself. "The papers probably won't carry the news in Chicago, and it's for sure Addie won't tell her. Then too, Addie didn't get here until the day after the murder. Maybe it'll be all right."

"Poor kid," offered Matt. He finished his eggs and got out his pipe, packing it with elaborate care. "She's probably scared to death."

"Scared, my foot. I'm sure she's enjoying it all immensely. She'll do everything possible to get in the way and gum up the entire investigation. Everything. I'll try to avoid her." Harrison sighed.

"Poor little kid," Matt repeated. "Well, so tell me, what *have* you got so far? You must have something to go on."

Harrison shook his head. "Practically nothing. Lucinda Jackson, age 24, occupation, teacher. Unmarried, no family that anyone knows of. Found strangled in her bed between the hours of 1 and 3 a.m. the morning of January first. No apparent motive, no witnesses. But you already know that from the morning news, I suspect. What do you think?"

"Strangled on New Year's. Seems peculiar."
Matthew chewed on his pipe.

"Could be. I just don't know enough yet. Correction, I don't know anything yet. That's why I want to get out there right away." He took a last gulp of coffee, and got up from the table.

"Mrs. Otto's School," said Matt in a reminiscent tone. "Funny, you know, I sometimes forget it's even there. All closed up in itself—all private and exclusive." Matthew had taken his pipe out of his mouth, crossed his long legs out in front of him under the table, and leaned back in his chair. It was a rare pose, and it meant that he was in a mood to talk, which was also unusual.

Something in his tone caught Harrison's interest. Impatient a moment ago to be on his way, he suddenly sat back down. He'd forgotten the older man had lived in Delenbridge for longer than anyone could remember.

"You've never been out there?" Matt was saying.

"No. I guess I should have, to visit Addie, but I never got around to it."

"Well," said Matt, "you're in for an experience. They're a queer bunch."

"What do you mean?"

"Well, Mrs. Otto herself, for one thing. It's twenty years since she came here and started that school. But nobody seems to really know anything about her—where she came from, who her husband was, that kind of thing. And you know the local gossips have tried to find out! But that woman doesn't open up to anybody."

Matthew continued. "Oh, she's polite all right. So damn polite she'll freeze you right up. Always lookin' down at you like you were some kind of insect, or like you just said or did exactly the wrong thing. I can't stand the woman!"

The latter comment was not surprising, since Matthew Gregory held the female sex in general in low regard. Mostly, however, his wrath was directed toward flirtatious women—"chattering squirrels," he called them. Mrs. Otto sounded like a very different type. Mrs. Otto did not sound like a chattering squirrel.

"She sounds," said Harrison, "rather formidable."

"Rather what?"

"Well, frightening."

"Oh yeah. I don't envy you havin' to talk to her. She'll scare you all right, if you let her. She likes having the upper hand, putting you in your place. Does it awful well, with that frosty way of hers."

Matt picked up his pipe and prepared to relight it, then stopped reflectively. "And then there's the rest of 'em," he said.

"The rest?"

"The teachers. Like I say, nobody in town sees much of any of them. Guess Mrs. Otto thinks they're all too good to associate with us commoners. But they're strange too. Some of 'em are *awful* strange. Not so cold, like Mrs. Otto. But

peculiar. Eccentric, I guess you'd call them."
Matthew gave a short laugh. "Or crazy."

He finished lighting his pipe and stuck it in his mouth, signalling that his mood for conversation had passed.

Chapter Four

"Crazy," Beatrice Withers was saying. "Don't you think so, Inspector Emery? People that would go around strangling other people? They must just be plain crazy. Don't you think so, Inspector?"

It was perhaps an hour later, still mid-morning. The day was surprisingly cloudless and fresh after the previous night's storm—one of those bright, chilly days one occasionally gets in mid-winter.

Mrs. Beatrice Withers was Harrison's second witness, and his first cooperative one. The first, Alex the gardener, had answered all questions in curt monosyllables and had denied having seen, heard, or known a single thing. On the way back from his visit to the gardner's house, Harrison had encountered Beatrice Withers picking up fallen branches and debris from last night's storm ("just tidying up, Inspector")—and had decided to interrogate her next. She was, he learned, the history instructor, and she had been with the school for more years than she wanted to admit. Looking at the determinedly made-up face, he guessed her age as somewhere near forty. She probably would have admitted to twenty-nine.

"Er, well, you may be right," he said in answer to her question. He wondered if there was something in one of Mrs. Withers' eyes. She kept blinking them at him.

"Did you know Miss Jackson well? She'd been here, I think Mrs. Otto said, about two years?"

"Something like that," Beatrice replied indifferently. "I didn't know her really all that well."

"She had no enemies that you know of? People who might wish her harm?"

"Well, nobody liked her. Oh dear, I shouldn't say things like that, should I? Now you'll suspect me. I should feel sorry, and say what a shame, and how we all loved her, shouldn't I?" Mrs. Withers tittered nervously. She reached up and tucked two stray hairs back underneath her gardening hat. "But, well, it's not secret, Inspector. Lucie wasn't, she wasn't exactly the most pleasant person in the world. Oh, she seemed so, at first. Went to a great lot of trouble to make a good first impression, so that people thought her charming, and bubbly—you know the sort of person I'm talking of. Very dramatic, waving her hands about when she told stories and all that—oh, and pretty, too. No question about that.

"But she was mean, Mr. Emery. Really truly

mean. She just loved making fun of people. For instance, Sarah Bow, the maid, who's the dearest person in the world. And she does worry so about being plump. Poor thing, all she has to do is look at a piece of pie and she gains a pound right there. *You* know the sort I mean. And she just can't resist eating things she shouldn't, and so she'll eat the pie and all the time be saying, 'Oh, I shouldn't eat this, I shouldn't eat that.' She feels so terribly guilty, you know. So Lucie, who was as thin as a bird, used to go around at dinner saying 'Oh, I shouldn't eat this, I shouldn't eat this,' whenever Sarah was there. She thought it was funny, you know. And it hurt Sarah's feelings quite terribly. Anyway, she was always doing things like that. She was mean," Mrs. Withers repeated. "Really mean.

"I know," she continued, "that it's terrible to say this, but I can't feel really and truly sorry about Lucie dying. I mean, people like that, people who are unpleasant and who make the world that much harder to live in—well, one just doesn't feel that sorry for them when they do die, that's all."

Mrs. Withers blinked again, and Harrison decided that there was really nothing in her eye at all. He had a vague, uncomfortable idea she was trying to be flirtatious.

"Oh, dear," she proceeded, "I'm saying the wrong things again—I always do that. And please, Mr. Emery, for heaven's sake, don't take any notice of what I said about Lucie teasing

Sarah. My goodness, anyone would think I was trying to make *her* look guilty, giving her a motive, you know. And of course, I wasn't. Sarah Bow would not hurt a flea. I was simply using her as an *example*." She gave Harrison an accusing look, as if he were attributing any number of evil motives to Sarah Bow, the maid.

"Er, uh, harrumph," said Harrison. "I understand your meaning, Mrs. Withers. Now, if you could just fill me in a little bit about what you were doing the night of December 31, exactly what you saw and heard. . . ."

"What's he doing out in the garden?" asked Gwyneth. "That's not a proper place to conduct an investigation." From their bedroom window on the second floor, Gwyneth, Addie and Phyllis had a perfect view of the garden.

"He's probably just questioning everybody," said Addie, "and happened to run into Mrs. Withers on his way out to see Alex or something. I'll bet he's sorry he did. I don't know why she always has to wear those awful hats just to go out in the garden and dig around. I wish we could hear what they're saying."

"I just hope he knows the proper questions to ask, that's all," sniffed Gwyneth.

"He's young," noted Phyllis. "Well, pretty young anyway. He's not handsome like Mr. Linn. But he has nice brown hair and, well, kind of an air about him. He doesn't really look like a policeman."

"Let *me* see." Gwyneth pushed past Phyllis and peered out the window.

"Don't push," complained Phyllis.

"Be careful." Addie glowered at Gwyneth. "Do you want them to see us? The only way we can learn anything is if no one notices us. If nobody thinks we suspect anything. Don't you see?"

"Miss Know-It-All," sulked Gwyneth, but she sat back from the window. They were all silent for a minute, watching the garden.

"On the other hand," mused Addie, "we can't learn anything if we can't hear. I want to hear!" She paused, her brow furrowed, thinking.

"Supposing," she continued, "supposing I went downstairs—out through the kitchen and around. See that big hedge? They wouldn't see me and I could hear everything from behind there." She hopped off the bed. "I'm going," she announced.

"Addie," said Phyllis, horrified. "What if you get caught?"

"I'm coming too," said Gwyneth, jumping up. "You always try to run everything."

"No, there's more chance of us being discovered that way. I've got to go alone. Or would you rather go—alone?" Gwyneth sat back down.

"If you see anything suspicious," said Addie, "close the curtains. If I look up and see them shut, I'll know something's wrong and I'll try to get back up here as soon as I can." With that she slipped out the door.

No one was in the hallway. Addie tiptoed down the stairs, into the kitchen, and outside.

Once in the garden, she stopped. She could see the inspector and Mrs. Withers talking, Mrs. Withers gesturing dangerously with a garden spade. But she couldn't quite catch the words. She edged closer, behind the hedge which lined the garden path.

Addie crouched motionless, like a rabbit waiting for a hawk to fly past. She watched the inspector's face closely through the branches in the hedge, then relaxed. He had seen nothing. She settled herself more comfortably, and found a better opening in the branches through which to peek.

"I can assure you, Inspector, I heard nothing," Beatrice was saying. "Nothing at all. As Mrs. Otto has probably already told you, she and I spent the evening home alone playing cards. Everyone else went out, to parties or something." She spoke resentfully. "Lucie came in about midnight, I know it was midnight because she said something about turning into a pumpkin, and danced up the stairs with one shoe off.

"You'd think," sniffed Beatrice, "that a person could simply come home, say goodnight, and go straight off to bed. But Lucie had to make a production out of everything."

"She didn't seem worried or upset? Are you sure she didn't say anything else?"

"Let's see. No, she certainly didn't seem worried or upset. I said something about her being home early. She started laughing, though what there was to laugh about I'm sure I don't know, and said she was afraid to stay out too late since she had to come home alone. 'You never know what sort of people might be out on a night like this—drunkards, murderers even,' she said. Honestly, always exaggerating, Lucie was. Besides, I never heard her worry about anything like that before—she was always gallivanting around at all hours of the day and night. Hmph!" said Beatrice Withers.

"At any rate we both, Mrs. Otto and I, went to bed soon after. And Lucie's bedroom is on the second floor, while both of ours are on the third, so neither of us would have heard her—unless she made a real racket, screamed or something."

"You both went up at the same time? How soon after Lucie?"

"No more than half an hour, I'm sure. The fire had gone out some time before, and it was cold. After Lucie came, we just finished up our game and went up."

"I see. And what about the others? What about Mr. Linn?"

"He wasn't in yet, no. I really can't say what time he came in—or if he did. He keeps terribly odd hours, Mr. Linn does, one can never keep track of him." Mrs. Withers paused. Harrison looked up from his notebook. Mrs. Withers giggled, and pushed the rebellious hairs back again under her hat. "I think really," she said, "that Mr. Linn is, oh, you know, sowing his wild oats. Not that anyone can blame him," as if Harrison were at this moment blaming him. "He's so handsome, and women just seem to follow him about. But he'll settle down one of these days."

A thought struck Harrison. "Was Lucie Jackson one of the women who 'followed him about'?" he asked.

Beatrice Withers stiffened. She drew herself up straight. "Certainly not, Mr. Emery. Or rather, she may have wished he'd pay her attention. That I don't know. Perhaps he did pay her some slight attention—of a purely superficial nature, of course. But Mr. Linn has standards—he knew what she was. He didn't need to waste his time on someone like her, pretty face or no." Beatrice Withers had turned red. "Certainly not."

"I see," said Harrison, his tone noncommittal. "Well, back to the night of the murder. Alex, the gardener, says he was in his house out back from early evening on. Can you by chance confirm that?"

"Well, all I know is that he was supposed to come in with wood for the fire, and he didn't. It went out by nine o'clock. But occasionally he does forget, and generally we go to bed earlier than midnight. But as to whether he was home, I really can't say. I assumed so."

"What of Sarah Bow—did you see or hear her? Was she out for the evening?"

"Now, Inspector, I *told* you I was simply using Sarah Bow as an example. Honestly, a person can't say anything at all in front of these policemen without them suspecting all sorts of things."

"Mrs. Withers," sighed Harrison, "I assure you I do not suspect anyone. All I am trying to do is get a clear idea of just where each person in the house was at the time of the death. That is all," he finished somewhat savagely.

"Well, all right. There's no need to get annoyed. Sarah went to a party at, I believe, the Smiths—they have the brown farmhouse just down the road. I heard her come in through the kitchen door earlier, oh, around 11:00, and I assume she went to bed. I didn't hear her after that."

"You 'heard' her? You didn't actually see her come in?"

"Why no, Inspector, Mrs. Otto had given her the night off. There was no need for her to check in with us at all. She probably just went straight to her room."

"I see," he said, and noted this down under the suspicious eye of Beatrice Withers. She did not, however, accuse him again of stacking the evidence against poor Sarah Bow, the maid. He straightened up from his notebook aware, thankfully, that he had reached the end of his list of questions for Mrs. Beatrice Withers.

"What happened?" asked Phyllis, as she opened the door and let Addie in. "You were lucky to get back up here in time. They left the garden right after you did."

"I know," said Addie calmly. "I knew they were about to wind things up. Uncle H had had about as much as he could take of Mrs. Withers." She sat down at the dressing table and, maddeningly, began to brush her hair.

"What *happened?*" demanded Gwyneth, stamping her foot.

"Oh, about what I expected. Mrs. Withers behaved in the usual way, fluttering around and talking too much. You know," decided Addie, pausing, "I think it would be fun to be a police investigator. I mean, for once the things people say would be interesting—instead of boring the way they usually are—because you'd be listening for something specific: clues.

"Take Mrs. Withers, for example," she continued. "She's a type, I think. If you were a policeman, you'd come across a lot of people like her. She was trying to cover something up—even I could tell that—but she didn't go about it the way most people would. Instead of just keeping quiet, she chattered on all the more about all sorts of things that she thought had nothing to do with the case. Just running on—probably trying to distract Uncle Harrison."

"But you know," she finished thoughtfully, "she gave away more than she knew, a lot more. And he knew it too." There was a hint of admiration in her tone.

"What kinds of things?" pursued Gwyneth.

"So far you haven't told us anything. Just not anything."

"All right." Addie held up her hand and bent down one finger. "First, she thinks, just like I did, that there was something between Mr. Linn and Miss Jackson. She denied it, but she thinks it all the same. And second, nobody knows where Mr. Linn was last night. He didn't come in till really late. She admitted that without thinking, and then looked like she was sorry she had said it. She was really trying hard to—I don't know—protect him or something. And she ended up making him look more suspicious than anyone. She's so obvious," scorned Addie. "She's probably feeling really proud that she convinced Uncle H that Mr. Linn is innocent."

"What else?" questioned Gwyneth as Addie paused in thought.

"Oh, let's see . . . not much. Oh, she didn't like Miss Jackson. She didn't like her at all. I didn't know that. I'd almost say . . . I'd almost say she must have hated her." Addie put down her hairbrush and cupped her chin in her hand. "I wonder. . ."

"So she was trying to protect Mr. Linn," said Phyllis, following a line of thought of her own. "Do you suppose she knows he did it, or just suspects?"

"Probably just suspects," said Addie. "You know how nervous and fluttery she is. If she really knew, I bet she'd have been lots more nervous. In fact, she'd probably have given the whole thing away."

"What do you suppose will happen now?" asked Gwyneth. "Is he still questioning people? Oh, I wish he'd question us. Wouldn't it be fun? Do you suppose he'll question you, Phyllis? You were there, after all."

"The police already did that the night of the murder. I told you." Phyllis tugged at a lock of hair. "They just asked me if I'd seen or heard anything. I said no, and Mrs. Otto said not to upset me, and, well, that was it."

"Grownups never think children know anything," said Addie. "Look how Uncle Harrison spent all that time with dumb old Mrs. Withers, and she doesn't know anything more than you do. He probably won't even ask you anything."

"We could get Sarah to tell us what questions he asked her," suggested Phyllis. "She'd tell us. Do you suppose your uncle is downstairs now asking questions? Maybe we could see if we went to the top of the stairs and looked down," she finished bravely.

Addie gave her a curious look. "I don't think we can risk it," she said. "There's one thing I haven't told you. . . ." She hesitated.

"Go *on,*" said Gwyneth.

"Well, when I was out there watching, I looked up, you know, to make sure that you hadn't shut the curtains. The first time I looked up, I thought you had, and I was really scared for a minute. But then I realized that it was the *third*-floor bedroom—Mrs. Otto's room—whose curtains were shut.

"Only," said Addie, "the next time I looked

up, Mrs. Otto's curtains were open. And Mrs. Otto was standing there at the window . . . looking down."

Gwyneth and Phyllis looked at her in horror. "Did she see you?" they both asked at once.

Addie picked up the hairbrush again, and pulled at its bristles, one by one. "I don't know," she said slowly, looking worried. "I don't know."

Chapter Five

Paul Linn sprawled lazily on the sofa, his feet on the coffee table. He smoked a cigarette, and from time to time flicked ashes in the approximate direction of the ashtray. He looked up as the door to the drawing room opened and Mrs. Otto walked in. She was dressed in a gray dress with no trimmings of any kind on it. She frowned when she saw Paul's feet on the table.

"So there you are, Lenore," he said. "I've been wondering where you'd gotten to."

"Put that out, please. I loathe the smell of smoke." She paced irritably back and forth across the room. "And what, may I ask, gave you the idea you could call me by my first name?"

"Nothing. It's just that I had a feeling it's the kind of thing that would annoy you. And I was right, wasn't I?" Paul Linn took another drag on his cigarette, leaned back, and blew smoke rings into the air. He watched Mrs. Otto walk to the

French doors and look out, then walk back to the mantel.

"You're roaming around a lot," he noted. "Like a nervous cat. A cat on a hot tin roof, as the saying goes. Are you a cat on a hot tin roof, Mrs. Otto?"

"I'm glad," snapped Mrs. Otto, "you are able to take all of this so lightly."

"One must take everything lightly, my dear," said Paul. "Everything. It's the only way to remain sane."

Mrs. Otto started, then turned the full force of her icy stare on him. "And you, of course, are perfectly sane."

Paul was unperturbed. "Now Mrs. Otto, that's not a tiny touch of sarcasm I hear in your voice, is it? I should think that you would be above that. After all, a person with your sense of decorum, your famous queenly poise? Where is your famous queenly poise, Mrs. Otto?"

Mrs. Otto seemed about to speak, then started again at a sound from outside. "Oh, it's Inspector Emery coming in from the garden." With one quick graceful movement she crossed over and opened the French doors out onto the patio. "This way's a bit quicker, Mr. Emery."

Harrison entered the drawing room, followed closely by a still-behatted Beatrice Withers.

"Inspector Emery, this is Mr. Linn. I told him to remain here, as I assumed you'd want to question him next."

"How do you do, Inspector?" Paul rose from

the sofa unhurriedly, and stuck out a hand. "Good morning, Beatrice. You look simply . . . stunning this morning. Must be the hat. As a matter of fact. . ."

Beatrice Withers put a hand to her head and tittered. "Have you finished questioning everyone else, Inspector?" Mrs. Otto added quickly.

"Almost. I haven't had a chance to talk to the maid yet, nor Mr. Linn. And I will need to ask you a few more questions before I leave, Mrs. Otto."

"Certainly," said Mrs. Otto. "Come along, Beatrice. We shall leave you and Mr. Linn alone. I'll tell Sarah Bow you'll be wanting to speak with her in a few minutes." Beatrice Withers reluctantly followed. The door shut quietly, leaving Harrison alone with the man who, thus far, seemed to be his chief suspect.

Now it was Paul Linn's turn to roam. He did it casually, sauntering from the fireplace to the French doors, and back again.

"Well, Inspector, ask away," said Paul with a wave of his hand. "Now the first thing you'll want to know, I suppose, is where I was at the time of the death. My alibi, in other words. Whether I can prove I was where I say I was. Right, Inspector?"

Harrison in the past had encountered witnesses who became so intimidated that they could not, out of fear or awe, utter a single word. Thus far, he reflected, he had experienced no such problem in this case.

"No one seems to know what time you came in on the night of New Year's Eve," Harrison began. "Or where you were."

"Oh, yes. I was sure you'd have heard that. Yes, I was mysteriously absent that evening. Didn't even show up for dinner. Didn't come back till all hours. Maybe didn't come back at all. Right? At least that would be roughly Mrs. Withers' version.

"At any rate, I suppose I must tell you where I was. But you must promise not to tell anyone," he lowered his voice to a conspiratorial whisper. "I was at a party." He paused. "But whose party, you may ask? Ah, you may well ask. For that is the secret." He blew two smoke rings, and admired them.

Harrison sighed. "Mr. Linn, if you don't mind. . ."

"I was at a party," continued Paul, "at the home of Jacob Willoughby. I am, Inspector, secretly engaged to marry Jacob Willoughby's daughter, Melissa."

Harrison could not quite cover up the startled expression on his face, and Paul let out a whoop of laughter. "So you know Melissa, Inspector?"

Harrison had met Melissa Willoughby on only one occasion, but he remembered her very well: thirty-two (or so) years of age, a whining voice, and hair as fine and thin as a balding cat's. Her father was reputed to be the richest, and most unpleasant, man in the county, and his daughter took after him.

Melissa Willoughby?

Paul spun around and faced Harrison with a grin. "Now, you won't give away my secret, will you, Inspector? I couldn't bear the gossip. And besides, it's not, er, quite official yet. I'm still trying to convince Jake Willoughby what a model son-in-law I'd make."

So that was it. And what if Paul Linn did "sow a few wild oats," as Beatrice Withers so coyly put it? What would Jacob Willoughby think of his son-in-law doing that? And what of Lucie Jackson. . .?

But Paul was still talking. "At any rate, leaving my motives aside, whatever you may think personally, marrying a woman for her money—and I'm not admitting I'm doing that—is not against the law. Back to my alibi.

"The party started at eight. I didn't want to get there too early—it takes a while for those stuffed shirts to get enough liquor in them to unbend, and until that happens it's dull. I also didn't want to suffer through another one of Sarah Bow's dinners. She's substituting for the cook during the holidays and my stomach can *not* take much more of it.

"So at five, I went down to Ben's Tavern and had a few beers and a sandwich. All they serve at those parties are those little canape things—cat food on toast. Plus, Jake Willoughby always has to show off by serving tons of *the* most expensive caviar. Place must reek of it for days after."

Paul settled back, enjoying his story. The fact

that he was being interrogated concerning a murder case did not seem to bother him in the slightest, and he certainly didn't seem much upset over Lucie Jackson's death. Paul continued. "Well, around nine, I took myself off to the party. It turned out to be one of the more successful ones, too. Let's see, Melissa had a rip-roaring fight with her father that'll keep the local gossips occupied for a week. Jake lost his temper but good, and fired the butler. I'm still unclear as to just what the butler had to do with it all. So the butler left in a huff, and then, horror of horrors, that left NO ONE TO SERVE THE HORS D'OEUVRES! Naturally, there was nothing for old Mrs. Willoughby to do but take herself off to bed with a case of hysterics.

"And since," finished Paul, "there was no one to serve the hors d'oeuvres, I fed them to the dog, who appreciated him. Although he was sick later," he added an an afterthought.

"Terrific party. I got quite involved in it, to tell you the truth, drank gallons of champagne, and stayed till the last Auld Lang Syne was sung."

"And what time was that?" questioned Harrison, who had not managed to get a word in for several minutes.

"Two-thirty, I believe. Something like that."

"Two-thirty? And you came home directly afterward?"

"Yes. The clock in the hall said a little after three when I got in." Paul Linn looked crestfallen. "I do apologize, Inspector, for joking about all this. Mrs. Otto is absolutely right. I don't take things seriously enough. Or perhaps," he mused, "I take them *too* seriously, and make jokes so as not to become too depressed." He paused, appearing to ponder the psychological workings of his mind.

"The night of the murder, Mr. Linn. . ." Harrison broke in, annoyed. "If you would think back, please. Was anyone up when you returned?"

"What? Oh no, not a soul," Paul said quickly. "Saw nothing, heard nothing. A damned shame, too. I went right up those stairs to the third floor. If I'd only just looked down the hall there at the second floor, maybe I'd have seen something . . . but I didn't. Nothing at all."

Nothing at all. They were like members of a Greek chorus, all chanting the same thing. Nothing at all, nothing at all. But, thought Harrison, there had been a murder, and a murder wasn't nothing. Strange that everyone in the entire house could sleep through a murder. Convenient. He didn't believe it.

"Were you well acquainted with Miss Jackson, Mr. Linn? Well enough to know, for example, whether she had any enemies? Anyone who might have had a reason to kill her?"

"I really didn't know her all that well," said Paul, echoing Beatrice Withers. "I haven't any idea at all who might have wanted to kill her. How could anyone think of such a thing?" He shuddered and raised his hands in a gesture of futility.

"Come now, Mr. Linn," said Harrison. "She was here for nearly two years. The school is very small. You had to have known her at least fairly well."

Paul hesitated fractionally. "Well, of course I knew her, Inspector. But I make it a point not to get any more personally involved with the people here than I have to. We see enough of each other as it is, what with meals and classes. We'd be at each other's throats. Besides, if you got involved with the people here, you'd be signing your own death warrant. Cause of death: drowning in a sea of gossip." He stopped. There had, after all, been a death.

"I really don't know who'd have wanted to kill Lucie, Inspector," he finished in a subdued tone. "I really don't."

"What sort of person was Lucie Jackson, Mr. Linn?"

The question apparently took Paul by surprise. "What sort of person? What do you mean, Inspector? What has that got to do with her murder? It was probably some maniac sneaking in here, killing for some insane reason. The victim could have been anybody, just happened to be Lucie. Don't you think that's what most likely happened?"

"Perhaps," said Harrison. "But I find, in any case, that it's always helpful to know something about the character of the victim. It often turns out to be the thing that solves the case. So, Mr. Linn . . . your impression of Lucie Jackson?"

Paul Linn lost some of his poise. "Well, I can't imagine anyone wanting to kill her. She was irritating sometimes. 'Put on airs,' as Sarah Bow would say. Always acting like she was the star in a play or something, always drawing attention to herself. It got to be a tiresome act. But you don't kill someone because she gets on your nerves," he finished lightly.

"No, I wouldn't imagine so," said Harrison. "And so, Mr. Linn, your relationship with Miss Jackson was nothing more than casual, is that right? Professional, you might say."

Paul hesitated. "Certainly, yes . . . professional."

"I see. Well, thank you, Mr. Linn. I think that will be all for now. I may be calling on you again."

Paul rose with relief, and stuck out his hand. Now that the interview was over, he regained some of his jauntiness. "Any time, Inspector, any time. Oh, and uh, you're not to give away my little secret, remember?" He winked as though he and Harrison shared a private, boyish joke.

When Paul had gone, Harrison sat down on the couch. He reached out a hand to ring for Sarah Bow, changed his mind and withdrew it. He sat thus for some moments, going over his notes and recalling, as was his custom, his witnesses' facial expressions, their pauses, the things they had not said as well as the things they had. In particular he remembered Beatrice Withers and her bristling, defensive reaction to the question of whether Lucie had been involved with Paul.

"So Paul Linn has no idea who'd want to kill Lucie Jackson?" Harrison muttered to himself, stroking his chin. "I don't think I quite believe that. I think that Paul Linn, for reasons of his own, wanted very much to have Lucinda Jackson out of the way. The question is, did he want it enough . . . to kill her?"

Harrison would have been very surprised had he known that at that moment upstairs, lying on a patchwork shepherdess quilt, his niece was pondering that very same question.

Chapter Six

Sarah Bow in her turn had just been ushered out of the drawing room, her account having generally concurred with that of Beatrice Withers. She had gone to a party, but had come home early and been in bed by 11:30. She had heard nothing after that. And no, she supposed that poor Lucie Jackson was not very well liked —she tended to hurt people's feelings (without meaning to, of course). But Sarah could think of no reason for anyone to kill her.

Mrs. Otto re-entered the room, pausing in the doorway. "Have you finished, Inspector?" She was looking pale and drawn from the flu, but held herself upright. Mrs. Otto, thought Harrison, was not one to give in to an illness . . . or to a crisis.

"Just one or two more things I'd like to ask you, if you don't mind." Mrs. Otto hesitated, then walked slowly over to the sofa and sat down. Harrison consulted his notebook.

"There were no signs of a forced entry into the house on the night of the murder. Were the doors always kept locked?"

"Certainly." Mrs. Otto folded her hands in her lap. "That was Sarah Bow's responsibility. However, on that night, I double-checked them myself."

"And do you generally do that?"

"If I happen to be the last one to go upstairs, yes."

Harrison had never met anyone before to whom the word "stately" applied so perfectly. Mrs. Otto was handsome. An odd word. Not beautiful. And yet her features were not in the least masculine, and her figure, though somewhat taller than average, was slim and graceful. With a different personality, she would have not been handsome . . . she would have been pretty. Harrison thought Mrs. Otto was handsome, stately, and very very cold. He suddenly found himself wondering what Addie thought of Mrs. Otto.

"Is there anything else, Inspector?"

Harrison started guiltily. He had the uncomfortable feeling that Mrs. Otto knew precisely what he had been thinking about. "Er, yes. How many people have keys to the house?"

"All the teachers, Sarah, and Ellen Gray, the cook. And myself, of course. That's all."

"That's quite a few keys."

"Ten." Mrs. Otto looked at him coldly. "These people do live here, after all. They need to have free access to and from the house."

"Yes, of course. It doesn't narrow things down much, however. A key could easily have been lost, or stolen."

"Or it could be that one of us here at the school is the killer. The owner of one of those ten keys. That's what you think, is it not, Inspector?"

"I'm afraid it does point to that, Mrs. Otto."

"I . . . see." They were silent a moment. Mrs. Otto picked up a porcelain figurine from the coffee table and turned it in her hands. Most women wore some sort of jewelry on their arms, but Mrs. Otto's hands were bare of rings and bracelets. She did not even wear a watch, and Harrison wondered if she were one of the people who always know what time of day it is, down to the minute. Mrs. Otto looked up, found Harrison watching her, and put down the figurine. She folded her hands in her lap. "And what else do you need to know, Mr. Emery?"

"The door to Miss Jackson's own room was found unlocked after the murder. Did she generally leave it unlocked at night, do you know?"

"I'm sure I have no idea, Inspector. The students' room do not have locks on them; the instructors' room do. For their own privacy, I certainly assumed they all used those locks."

"I see. Did anyone else have a key to Lucie's room?"

"I have keys to all the rooms. No one else."

"How did you happen to hire Lucie Jackson, Mrs. Otto?"

If Mrs. Otto was surprised by the question, she did not show it. "She requested an interview, saying she had just graduated from college and was looking for a position in the area. Her credentials were impeccable, and I was in need of a dance teacher at the time."

"What were her credentials?"

"A major in drama and a minor in dance. I believed that the combination of drama and dance would be a good one for the girls. I cannot afford to hire many teachers, and if one person can teach in two subject areas it is a definite advantage. She had taught children's theater classes to earn tuition money. I was impressed by her ambition, as well as her experience in working with children."

"Her family must not have been wealthy, then, if she had to work to pay for her schooling. And to take a job immediately after graduating."

"Lucinda was an orphan," said Mrs. Otto shortly. "She had no brothers and sisters, and her parents were both killed in an auto accident when she was quite young. When she interviewed for the position here, she told me that she had been raised by a grandmother who had died a few years before, leaving her no money at all. I gathered that the grandmother was quite unpleasant and tyrannical, and that Lucinda was not happy with her. I did not question her further."

"I see. That may explain a few things, then."

"Explain what?"

"The fact that nothing of a particularly personal nature was found in Lucie's room. I wondered about the lack of photographs, letters from family or friends, things of that sort. If she was an orphan, that explains part of it. But what about friends? Did she have any male friends, for example?"

Mrs. Otto hesitated. "I'm sorry, Inspector, I really don't know. Lucinda did not confide in me. There were a few young people in town, artists and would-be actors most of them, that she seemed to be friendly with. In fact, I believe it was one of them whose party she went to. But I know nothing whatever about them."

"Do you know the name of that friend? The one whose party she went to?"

"Not off-hand. But I can find it for you."

"What about the other teachers? Was Lucie particularly close to any of them?"

"I have told you, Inspector, Lucinda did not confide in me."

"Did you like Lucie Jackson, Mrs. Otto?"

Mrs. Otto raised her eyebrows fractionally. "Like her?" she said, as one might speak to a child who had asked a particularly foolish question.

"Well. . ." Harrison felt that he *had* asked a foolish question. He could not imagine Mrs. Otto liking anyone. Liking, or disliking, implied feeling. And yet. . .

The faint surprise Mrs. Otto had evinced at the question was replaced by her usual impassive expression. She replied smoothly. "Lucinda was very charming initially. As time went on, she began to display some rather annoying habits. She did not take her job seriously, and I began to feel that she was far too self-centered to become a really good teacher. Also, I think she felt quite stifled here, perhaps resented being forced into a teaching job when she had ambitions of acting. I doubt whether she would have stayed with the school much longer. And, I must admit, I would not have been sorry to see her leave."

"Mrs. Otto," Harrison finally asked in despair, "didn't *anyone* like Lucie Jackson?"

This time the eyebrows really went up. Mrs. Otto did not approve of Inspector Harrison Emery, or his methods, or his questions. She made that clear without saying a word, and even more clear when she finally did speak. "I'm sure I do not know, Inspector Emery," said Mrs. Otto.

"I, er, think I'll be on my way for now. I'm waiting for some lab reports to come through. They ought to be ready just about now. Thank you for your time, Mrs. Otto . . . and your cooperation. I guess I ought to say hello to my niece, as long as I'm here."

"Must you?" Mrs. Otto asked shortly. She hesitated. "I am hoping to keep this as quiet as possible, and to have it cleared up quickly, for the sake of the school." She took a deep breath. "Only two other students besides Adelaide are back, and the others should not be returning for another two or three days. That gives you a little time. I don't want the three who are here upset by all this, but also, I must admit I don't want them gossiping among themselves—going to their parents with stories that they are bound to exaggerate. You haven't visited Adelaide since she's been here. There's certainly no reason why you should need to do so now, is there?"

"I can understand how you feel, Mrs. Otto. Certainly I can see Addie another time. It's not as if talking with her has any bearing on the case, after all."

There was a discreet tap at the door. Sarah Bow entered, looking apprehensively at Harrison and circling him like a shy dog.

"Excuse me, ma'am. There's a phone call for you. Mrs. Applegate, I'm afraid. Jane's mother. She's fearfully upset. She says she won't send Jane back until the murderer is found *and* punished. She says she won't have a murderer running about loose. She demands to talk to you."

Mrs. Otto looked at Harrison with a smile that wasn't even icy any more, only tired. "So it's beginning already. How foolish I was to think I could keep it quiet. Most of the girls come from other states, you see, and I thought. . ." her voice trailed off. With a slight squaring of her shoulders, she rose and turned to the distracted Sarah. "Tell Mrs. Applegate I'll be with her in a moment. I'll walk with you to the door, Inspector."

Paul appeared from nowhere to join them in

the hallway, and Harrison wondered briefly if he had been listening at the door.

"All finished, Inspector?"

"For now, yes, thank you."

At the door, Mrs. Otto hesitated. "You know, Inspector, Lucinda did get a few letters now and then. And now that I think of it, she did have an old notebook she used to write in occasionally. I assumed it was mostly drama notes, but I don't know. You haven't mentioned that book, so I assume it wasn't found."

"No, it certainly wasn't."

"Well, perhaps she had already thrown it away. And undoubtedly it wasn't important. Well, Inspector, I must answer that phone call."

"Good-bye, Mrs. Otto. Mr. Linn."

Harrison walked the tree-lined driveway back to his car, preoccupied. He did not at first notice that he was being followed. A twig cracked, breaking his concentration.

"Who's there?" he called out.

"Ssh!" said Addie, appearing from behind a tree. "Do you want to get me into trouble? I had a hard enough time sneaking out here without you yelling like that. Hello, Uncle H. I haven't seen you for a long time. Have you arrested anyone yet?" She cocked her head to one side like an intelligent sparrow.

"Addie! I might have known. Now, listen. You are not to get involved in this. Mrs. Otto didn't want me to talk to you for fear of upsetting you. And she was absolutely right. Er . . .

your mother doesn't know about any of this, does she?"

Addie carefully smoothed the ribbon on her yellow dress. "Nope," she replied. "Are you kidding? She'd make me go straight home if she did, and send me to George Washington Junior High. No, luckily she just put me on the plane by myself yesterday. I called her last night and told her I got here safely and was fine—which is perfectly true. Darn it. I wish I'd come down one day sooner, so I've had been here when Miss Jackson was killed. I bet I'd have noticed more than Phyllis. But I think I can help anyway."

"Wait a minute. Phyllis? She was the only student who was here the night of the murder, right? She was asleep at the time."

"Yes. I don't see," said Addie, "why everyone else gets questioned and we don't. It's not fair."

Harrison sighed. "I knew it. I just knew you were going to get in on this somehow. All right. Just how do you think you can help?"

Addie dragged him back away from the walk. "Somebody might see us," she explained in a whisper. "Well," she began, "I just happened to be outside when you were questioning Mrs. Withers." Harrison shot her a look, and she hurried on. "Well, *she's* certainly no good. She obviously thinks Mr. Linn did it, and she's always making sheep eyes at him so I know she was trying to protect him. Anybody could see that. And as for the others, well, how do you know any of them are reliable? Whereas, *I* am. I obviously didn't kill Miss Jackson, I wasn't even here. And I'm certainly not in love with Mr. Linn, so I wouldn't want to be protecting him or anybody else. Plus, I know all kinds of things about the school that you certainly couldn't know unless you lived here. Little things. Sometimes some little thing that nobody thinks is important *is* important, isn't that true?"

"True," admitted Harrison.

"And last of all, I knew Miss Jackson, and you didn't. And Miss Jackson was acting funny last term, there at the end."

"Funny? How do you mean?"

"It's hard to explain. Miss Jackson, well, talked a lot, and most of the things she said were just silly. She'd say things she thought we wouldn't understand—and then be secretive, and wouldn't explain what she meant. I guess she was trying to impress us or something. Most of what she said was just talk—just nothing. And so nobody paid very much attention.

"But she said something right before vacation about not being around here much longer."

"She did?" Harrison's attention was captured.

"It might not mean anything. I mean, Miss Jackson was always talking about how old-fashioned and provincial this place was (she used words like that: 'pro-vin-cial') and how she couldn't wait to get away. But this time, she acted like she really meant it. Like she had a secret. A real secret."

"Is there anything else you can think of, Addie? This might be important."

"I've been trying to think. There was one

thing, but it's hard to tell. Even I could never be sure, really, whether Miss Jackson was saying something serious or just saying something silly to be dramatic. But around that same time, we were talking about money, and being rich. And Miss Jackson said anybody could have money, if he just knew the right way to go about it. And of course, somebody asked her what she meant, but she just laughed. You see what I mean? That could be a clue, or it might not be a clue at all.

"Darn it," said Addie, "I wish I'd been there the night of the murder. It's funny Phyllis didn't hear anything. It makes sense that the others didn't—they were all out, or asleep on different floors. But Phyllis was right there on the same floor. I just know that if I'd been there instead of her, I'd have seen something, I'd have felt that something was going to happen—I'd have known it. I bet you!"

"And I'll bet," said Harrison, looking at the small, bright eyes of his niece, "that you're probably right. Well, Addie, to continue our investigation, I'll ask you the same question I've asked everyone else. Can you think of anyone who might have had a reason to kill Miss Jackson?"

"Mr. Linn," said Addie promptly. "He was my choice from the very beginning, and we even asked the Ouija board, and it agreed. But now I'm not so sure. I mean, if Mrs. Withers suspects him, then that means that it's too obvious. But I *am* pretty sure that Miss Jackson was in love with him, and that there was something going on. She flirted with him, and when he'd get annoyed she'd act like she knew he didn't mean it. I don't know how to describe it. I just had the feeling they were having an AFFAIR. And if he denies it, then he's probably lying."

"I had that feeling too," mused Harrison. "He did deny it, as a matter of fact."

"But if Mr. Linn *didn't* do it," said Addie, "then I don't know who did. It's such a peculiar thing to happen, a murder. You wouldn't think Mrs. Otto would even allow it."

"Now what in the world do you mean by that?"

"I was being funny," Addie explained. "But really, it's kind of true. Here, everything is always just exactly the way it's supposed to be. Everybody knows just the proper fork to use, and the proper way to walk, and sit, and everything. You're never supposed to fidget, or touch your face, or fiddle with your hair, because that's unladylike—those are the sorts of things we worry about. Everything is *very* proper—and very dull. And now, a murder, and a scandal. Oh, I'll bet Mrs. Otto just hates it. I'll bet she's just seething. How's she going to explain this to everybody's parents, who sent their children here so they could impress their friends with how exclusive it is! A murder! Oh, wow! I wish, I really wish I knew what Mrs. Otto was thinking about it all."

"Addie, about Mrs. Otto. . ."

There was a movement behind the trees, and Harrison observed the bulky figure of Alex the gardener going from the house toward the gate. "Uh oh, I'd better go before somebody sees me," said Addie jumping up.

"Wait a minute, Addie," said Harrison, assuming what he hoped was a stern, uncle-ish tone. "Now listen, I don't want you getting involved in this. No more spying. No more listening in. Do you understand? This isn't some kind of game. I want you to stay completely out of it."

Addie brushed her blonde hair out of her eyes. She gave him her best smile. "Of course, Uncle Harrison."

Gwyneth leaned as far out of the window as she could. "Well, there he goes. Nothing much to see. He's just getting into his car—and now he's driving away. He's not carrying anybody away in handcuffs," she said, disappointed. "He must not have found anything out. I don't see Addie anywhere. I wonder if she got a chance to talk to him."

Something caught Phyllis' eye. "Quick! Get back from the window!" She pulled at Gwyneth's arm. "Look. Here comes Mrs. Withers across the lawn. She might see you."

Gwyneth stood back and started to close the curtains, then paused. "She's acting . . . funny."

"She always acts funny."

"No, I mean . . . sort of furtive. What's that she's carrying? It looks like a box or something."

"She is acting funny," Phyllis agreed. "Like she doesn't want to be seen. You can never tell about Mrs. Withers. We'll have to tell Addie."

Chapter Seven

"Yes, Lucie Jackson was at my party." The tall, bearded figure who answered Harrison's knock looked like a latter-day Daniel Boone. "I wondered whether I ought to come to you, now you've saved me the trouble of deciding. Come in."

"Why did you think you ought to come to me?" asked Harrison.

"It's probably nothing," said Daniel Boone nervously. "It was just something Lucie said to me just before she left the party."

"Go on."

"Well, I was urging her to stay, things were just getting started. It was early, not even midnight, not even the new year. But she said no, she had to leave—that she had something else to do. She said . . . she said, 'My night is just beginning.' Something in the way she said that was, strange. Almost as if. . ."

"As if?"

"As if," said the man, pulling at his beard, "as if she were planning to do something . . . cruel and was going to enjoy it!"

Chapter Eight

"Phyllis," said Gwyneth, "you're putting your hair up all crooked."

It was five o'clock that afternoon. The beginning of the longest hour of the day. The girls were supposed to be reading, or resting, or washing their socks, or doing something constructive, before six o'clock dinner. They usually spent the hour in their room, bored.

They were bored now. Phyllis was fussing with her hair, Gwyneth was thumbing through a magazine. Addie lay on her back on the top bunk, her arms folded under her head, looking up at the ceiling.

Phyllis picked up the hand mirror, looked in it, and sighed. "I don't know why it always turns out this way."

"Maybe it just needs to grow out a little more," Gwyneth consoled. "Besides, it doesn't look *that* bad. It's supposed to look, you know, carefree and a little disarranged. That's the style."

"But not *crooked*. It's not supposed to look *crooked*." Phyllis gave up and started to take out the hairpins. She sighed. "I don't suppose Mrs. Otto would let me wear it that way anyway."

"Not for regular," said Gwyneth, "but she might for parties and things. Why don't you try it again. It would be good practice."

"All right," said Phyllis. She picked up the hairbrush and a handful of pins. "Addie? What are you thinking about?"

"I'm not thinking about anything," said Addie, not taking her eyes away from the ceiling. "I'm listening."

"Listening? To what?"

"Don't you hear it?"

"I don't hear anything," said Gwyneth testily.

"It's footsteps. In Mrs. Otto's room, above us. Mrs. Otto is pacing."

The three girls were quiet. "Hear her?" whispered Addie. "She's going from the door, over to the window, then back to the door."

The sounds were audible then, in the silence. A soft push-push-push on the ceiling.

"What do you suppose," said Addie, "she's going to do about all this?"

"What do you mean?"

"Well, that's the question she asked herself, after she took the Ouija board away from us. 'What am I going to do now?' Here she has this ex-clu-sive school with its impeccable reputation, and all of a sudden there's a murder, smack in the middle of everything. A murder isn't ex-actly going to get a lot of good publicity. A murder isn't exactly going to attract a lot of students. Besides, the murderer's still running around loose."

Phyllis shivered.

"Well," said Gwyneth reasonably, "what can she do?"

"That's probably why she's pacing—worrying. One thing she's probably trying to decide is whether to tell our parents. And the parents of the students who haven't come back yet."

"Well, she hasn't told my mother," said Gwyneth. "My mother'd be here right now if she had, or at least calling and being hysterical."

"Maybe Mrs. Otto is hoping it will all blow over," said Phyllis. "Hoping that the parents won't hear about it, or that if they do, they'll still send their children. Do you suppose?"

"Maybe."

"Addie," said Phyllis as the thought struck her, "you mean Mrs. Otto might have to close down the school?"

"Yes. Especially if the murderer isn't found right away."

"Oh," whispered Phyllis, "I wouldn't like that. I don't want to go away." The corners of her mouth began to tremble. She put down her hairbrush, her hair half finished.

When Phyllis cried, she cried gallons of tears and she cried for hours. She didn't mean to. She simply couldn't help it. The thing to do was to stop her before she really got started.

"Don't worry," said Addie quickly. "That's not going to happen."

"Don't worry," echoed Gwyneth. "It will be all right. We already know it was probably Mr. Linn. All Addie's uncle has to do is prove it. And Addie says he's very good. He's sure to solve the case in no time at all."

"Of course he will," said Addie. "Particularly with us helping him."

Phyllis dried her tears. "That's so," said Phyllis. "I hadn't thought of that." She smiled.

"Don't worry, Phyllis," said Gwyneth. "Let's talk about something else. I'll tell you about the article I've been reading. It says you can tell what people are like if you know what their favorite colors are. It says it's much more accurate than astrology."

"That's ridiculous," said Addie from the bed.

Gwyneth ignored her. "For example," she said, "my favorite color is yellow. That means I'm very feminine and graceful. I might be a dancer. I'm cheerful, but I have a mind of my own. I'm dainty." Gwyneth smoothed the folds of her new lace-edged velour dressing gown.

"Well," said Addie, "you're certainly not cheerful. And besides, those are all good things. There must be something bad too."

"Well," said Gwyneth, irritably, "It does say I'm selfish and that I don't like to be wrong."

"I knew it said something bad," said Addie.

"Miss Know-It-All," said Gwyneth, not cheerfully.

"What's your favorite color, Addie?" asked Phyllis through a mouthful of hairpins.

"I don't have one," said Addie.

"You must have one," insisted Phyllis.

"Well, all right then. Red."

Gwyneth consulted the magazine. "You're intelligent but you like to shock people and you swear."

"I do not."

"Well, that's what it *says*. You like words. You have a passionate nature, and you get angry easily."

"I don't think I'm passionate," said Addie, "though I can't say for sure. But I certainly don't get angry. When have I ever gotten angry?"

"Well, I'm just telling you what it *says*. What's your color, Phyllis?"

"Pink."

"Pink. Let's see. You're feminine, too, like me, but you're also gentle. It doesn't say anything about me being gentle. You like animals and flowers. You're shy, and you hate being the center of attention." Gwyneth looked up from the page. "That's all true, Phyllis. Every bit. Also, it says you tend to be gullible, you're a conformist, and a mystic."

"What's that?" asked Phyllis.

"It means," said Addie from the bunk, "that you believe everything people tell you, and you follow rules, and you believe in magic and the Ouija board and things like that."

"Yours is just right, Phyllis. You are pink, exactly."

"What happens if she changes her mind to green someday?" said Addie.

"It doesn't say. I guess she'd just have to change her personality, that's all. You should change to green, Addie. You're more like green. Green is intelligent, intuitive, questioning, and independent. And green does *not* get angry. Green is placid."

"Red sounds more like Mr. Linn," offered Phyllis.

"You're right, Phyllis," agreed Addie. "Mr. Linn certainly can get angry. And I would imagine that he's terribly passionate."

"Mrs. Withers sounds like violet," said Gwyneth. "Violet is pretentious, and inquisitive, that means nosey. And violet wears bright colors, and talks too much."

"Is there a gray?" Addie asked suddenly.

Gwyneth consulted the page. "No. Why? Nobody would choose gray for a favorite color."

"Well," said Addie, "Mrs. Otto reminds me of a gray. Not a mousy sort of gray. A kind of steel gray, but pretty. With a hint of silver in it."

"Why silver?" asked Phyllis. She looked at herself in the mirror, finally satisfied with the results.

"I don't know really. I guess because she's so elegant, and silver is elegant. And silver seems cold, but kind of fragile too."

"Mrs. Otto certainly isn't fragile," said Gwyneth.

"No, I suppose she isn't really. It's just that sometimes I think that maybe, way deep inside, she is." Addie looked up at the ceiling again, but the footsteps had stopped.

Chapter Nine

It was late that night, nearly midnight. Everyone at the school had either just dropped nicely off to sleep or had been sleeping for some time, when Sarah Bow's shrieks woke the house.

"Help!" cried Sarah Bow from her bedroom below the kitchen. "Police, help!" Receiving no immediate response, she screamed louder.

Mrs. Otto and Beatrice Withers, both in bathrobes, reached the second floor landing at the same time. They looked at each other anxiously. "You don't suppose," whispered Beatrice, ". . . the murderer?" She was pale and looked on the verge, herself, of shrieking.

"No. I'll go down and see what it is. No," she repeated, as Beatrice began to follow her, "you stay here and call Inspector Emery." She gave Beatrice an irritated little shove toward the phone at the end of the hall. "Call him!" she hissed, and hurried down to the kitchen.

Harrison reached the driveway of Mrs. Otto's school some minutes later. Not knowing what to expect, given Mrs. Withers' hysterical phone call ("another murder, Inspector, I'm sure of it—only it can't be Sarah who was murdered because she's screaming—at least I don't think it can be her"), he had prepared himself for the worst.

Mrs. Otto, changed now into a soft dress of her characteristic gray, opened the door. "Hello, Inspector, how good of you to come so quickly. I'm afraid Beatrice alarmed you unduly. There hasn't been another murder. Still, I'm glad you're here." She guided him into the drawing room. "Something *has* happened."

An odd sight greeted him. Sarah Bow, encased in a pink quilted robe and wearing enormous pink fuzzy slippers, sat sobbing loudly on the sofa. Beatrice sat on one side, Paul on the other, both trying without much success to calm her.

"A man!" cried Sarah Bow when she saw Harrison. "In my room. A man! Oh, I know as sure as I'm sitting here he meant to kill me." And she lapsed into fresh sobs.

"What happened to him?" asked Harrison. But Sarah Bow could do no more than point vaguely and wail.

"I think he escaped through the kitchen door," said Paul. "I came down as soon as I heard Sarah scream, and saw that the door was open, which it certainly shouldn't have been. So

I went right out to look. Didn't see anyone, though."

"That's right, Inspector," confirmed Beatrice. "I stopped upstairs to call you, and when I got downstairs Mrs. Otto was just bringing Sarah up from her room and Mr. Linn was just coming in from outside. Sarah was shrieking and shrieking."

Harrison turned to Sarah Bow, who appeared to have calmed down a shade. She nodded her head vigorously at Beatrice's words. "That's right," she said. "Shrieking and shrieking." Her curls shook with the emphasis of each word. Even the tips of her furry pink slippers trembled with excitement.

"Can you tell me exactly what happened, Miss Bow?"

"I was sleeping," she began, "and something woke me . . . a noise. I looked up, still half asleep, you know, and there was a man standing by my desk. He was bent over, I think, with his back to me. I never did see his face."

Mrs. Otto interjected. "Sarah was so upset we thought at first she might have had a nightmare. But the desk in her room had definitely been disturbed. Sarah said she had put everything away, and it was quite in disorder. You can look if you like."

"I will. Right now, as a matter of fact. One more thing, Sarah. Could you tell what he was wearing? A coat, for instance?"

Again the curls shook. "I just don't know, Inspector."

"Are you sure it was a man you saw? Could it have been a woman?"

"I never thought of that. I just somehow had the impression of a man. But it could have been a woman, I suppose." She turned to him imploringly. "Why did he choose me? Why my desk? I don't have anything anyone would want. . . ."

"Well, that's what we hope to find out. If you'll come with me, Miss Bow, we'll have a look."

"I'll come too, Mr. Emery," said Paul Linn, helping Sarah Bow to her feet. "After you've seen the room, I'll show you where I went outside. Hope I didn't ruin any clues for you, stumbling about. Footprints and all. Guess I should have thought before I went dashing out like that."

"All right," said Harrison. He turned to Beatrice and Mrs. Otto. "I'd like you both, if you will, to check the second and third floors. See if anything seems out of order. Addie, and the other two girls, where are they?"

"I told them to stay in their rooms," Mrs. Otto said. "I didn't want them upset."

"Better check on them too." He started toward the kitchen. Sarah Bow, leaning on Paul Linn's arm, followed reluctantly.

"No, I'm sure, Inspector. Nothing's been taken. See, here's my jewel box, not even touched. And I don't have anything like what you were talking about, no important papers or documents."

Harrison searched the desk himself. There seemed to be nothing but snapshots of assorted bucktoothed children (presumably nieces and nephews), ragged recipe clippings, and a few letters. Straightening up, he said, "Well, whatever he was looking for, he apparently didn't find it here." He paused. "Were you responsible for cleaning all the rooms, Miss Bow?"

She looked surprised. "Yes."

"Including the bedrooms, the teachers' rooms? Miss Jackson's room?"

Sarah Bow's eyes widened. "Yes."

"Did you ever take anything from Miss Jackson's room? A letter perhaps, a photo, something like that?"

Sarah Bow turned saucer eyes toward Paul Linn. "Is he accusing me of being a thief?" She turned to Harrison. "Are you accusing me of being a thief? I never took anything from anyone's room." The curls shook so furiously they seemed in danger of flying off her head.

"Excuse me, Miss Bow, I didn't mean to imply anything like that. I only meant that it seems obvious the man—whoever he was—was looking for something in your desk. I'm wondering if it ties in with Lucie Jackson."

He paced the room, talking as if to himself. "We never found anything in Lucie Jackson's room that told us about her life. No snapshots of family, no letters to friends. If someone thought that you had found that kind of evidence . . ."

He turned back to Sarah Bow. "Did Lucie ever give you anything like that? Or did you ever see pictures, letters, on her bulletin board, for instance? Please think hard."

"I already have, Inspector. Mrs. Otto already asked me about that after Lucie was killed. Lucie was always tacking up play programs and movie pictures—it was an actress she wanted to be, not a teacher—but I don't remember seeing anything else."

"All right, then," sighed Harrison. "I guess that's all for now. Why don't you go back into the drawing room, Sarah? And if you could come with me, Mr. Linn?"

They went up to the kitchen.

"Was this door generally kept locked at night?"

"Oh, sure," said Paul. "That was Sarah's responsibility, and she took it seriously. She was always nervous about prowlers and things, especially after the murder. Although I suppose she could have forgotten—I questioned her about it when I found it open, before you came, and she couldn't swear she'd locked it.

"I'm afraid I probably botched up whatever clues there were," apologized Paul, pointing to the doorknob. "See, those will all be mostly my fingerprints. And those are my footprints outside."

"Well, there's probably not much out here,

anyway. And the ground's pretty gravelly for footprints," said Harrison. "Here's some, though. Must be the gardener's. They look as if they lead out to his house."

"Must be," agreed Paul. "He came in for dinner."

"No lights on. Is he out? Or sleeping? I guess we'd better find out."

In the dark, perfectly trimmed trees and shrubbery were starkly silhouetted. Alex Campbell obviously tended the garden at Mrs. Otto's School for Girls as carefully in winter as in summer.

Alex Campbell was—or rather had been—asleep. He shuffled to the door in his bathrobe and answered all questions put to him in a surly manner. "No, I didn't hear anything. No, I didn't see anybody. What are you asking me for, aren't you the one that's supposed to be the cop?" After a brief and thoroughly uncooperative interview he proceeded to slam the door in Harrison's face.

"Mustn't mind him," said Paul Linn as they walked back to the house. "He's like that always —especially with police. Nothing personal, he just hates them all. He's not bad, really." Paul opened the kitchen door for the inspector. Then he gave a sharp cry. "Say, what's this?" Paul bent down and picked up a small object which lay just inside the kitchen door. "Well, what do you know, Inspector," he caroled, "a clue! Now

I want you to remember, if this turns out to solve the case, that I found it. Makes up for my footprints, wouldn't you say?"

"It" was a tiny copper pin in the shape of a star, old and tarnished. Harrison took it from Paul, and held it up between thumb and forefinger. "Hmm," he said. "Well."

"What is this all about, Inspector?" demanded Mrs. Otto as Harrison and Paul Linn re-entered the drawing room. "Sarah says you've been implying that the man in her room was Lucie's murderer. Is this true?"

"I don't know, it could have been a burglar. Although it doesn't seem like an ordinary burglary attempt to me."

He held out the star. "Do any of you recognize this?"

Sarah Bow gave a tiny gasp. "You found that in my room?"

Harrison looked at her. "No, in the kitchen, as a matter of fact. So you do recognize it?"

"No, oh no," Sarah Bow said. "I mean, I thought for a moment it looked familiar—but it doesn't, no, not at all. . . ." She looked away.

"Why, of course it looks familiar, Sarah," said Beatrice Withers, stepping forward. "It's something off that awful old Army jacket that Alex always wears. Thinks himself a war hero, he does."

"You know, she's right," put in Paul. "I didn't think of it at first, but it does look like something from Alex's jacket. He wears it all the time in the garden."

"Would he have been wearing it in the kitchen tonight? At dinner!"

"Are you kidding?" grinned Paul. "That ratty thing? I don't think it's been cleaned since World War II. Mrs. Otto wouldn't let him in the house with it on. Mrs. Otto," he said lightly, "insists upon proper attire." He gave her a sideways look, which she ignored.

"I see," said Harrison. "Well, it's probably nothing important. I think that's all I need for now. I'll have a patrol car drive by on the hour to make sure things are all right. But I don't think you'll have further disturbances tonight. Mrs. Otto? Perhaps you'll see me to the door?"

"What's going on, Inspector?" Mrs. Otto asked quietly when they were out of earshot of the others.

"I'm not sure. Can you think of any reason why Alex should snoop through Sarah's things? If it was Alex, that is?"

"No reason at all, I'm afraid. I don't know Alex well. He's not very pleasant, but he is the best gardener to be had."

"What were his feelings toward Lucie Jackson? Do you know?"

"No, I don't really. That's something Sarah would probably know, though. She's the only one who gets along with him at all."

"Is that so?" said Harrison.

"Do you really think this incident is related to Lucie's murder? Do you think Alex killed Lucie?"

"I don't know, Mrs. Otto. I'm going to do some checking in the morning, and then I'll be out again to ask a few more questions of Sarah and Alex. And—please don't worry. We're doing all we can."

When she heard the front door latch, Addie tiptoed back from the top of the stairs to her bedroom. She shut her door just as quietly as Mrs. Otto had shut the one downstairs. "Well, he's gone," she announced. "Gone until morning."

"What do you think?" asked Phyllis.

"Well, he suspects Alex. But he's being cautious about it. He's not convinced."

"But," said Gwyneth in a quiet voice, "*we* know who really did it. We saw it all. As soon as Sarah started to scream. We looked out our window and we saw Mr. Linn running out of the house, not at all as if he were chasing a prowler. . . ."

"But as if he were the one being chased," finished Addie. "I know."

Chapter Ten

The following morning, Thursday, Harrison was up and in his office early. He carried a mug of coffee to the file room and checked through to see what, if anything, he could find on Alex Campbell.

He hadn't given a thought to Addie and had had taken her promise that she would not interfere in the case seriously. Thus he would have been astonished had he known that she had taken not the slightest heed of his warning and had been listening to every possible scrap of conversation that had taken place the night before. He would have been even more astonished had he known that at this very moment Addie was searching through Paul Linn's closet. If Paul had found what he was looking for in Sarah Bow's room, Addie wanted to know about it.

"You shouldn't do it," Gwyneth had said righteously. "You should tell your uncle."

"I know. I will. But," Addie had argued, "Mr. Linn doesn't have any idea that we know. He won't be suspecting us. But if I call Uncle H now and he comes over, well, Mr. Linn might get nervous and destroy whatever it is he was trying to find in Sarah's room. The situation calls for a spy. Besides, there's no time to lose."

"Well, it's your neck," said Gwyneth in the manner of one washing one's hands of an affair. But her eyes had lighted with excitement.

I don't even know what I'm looking for, Addie complained to herself. She discovered the hidden cache of brandy, but doubted that it had any bearing on the case. Paul Linn's bureau drawers were a shambles, and the closet wasn't much better. It accounted for his habitually rumpled look which, somehow, was attractive on him.

Now where would I put something if I were Mr. Linn and wanted to hide it? Addie asked herself. She sat down on the edge of Paul Linn's bed and concentrated. Receiving no immediate inspiration, she jumped up again and paced about the room, looking behind mirrors and under books. If she could only know what she was looking for. . . .

Addie stopped in horror. She heard voices . . . but from where? And one of those voices was Paul Linn's. She had seen him go out . . . she had thought herself completely safe.

She stood frozen against the wall. There was nothing she could do. He must be out in the hall, he must be coming toward his door. He would open his door and he would find her. . . .

"Yes, Mr. Linn, I thought that would be you. I do hate to play games, but you see, I wasn't sure you'd come otherwise."

That was Mrs. Withers' voice. Not sure you'd come? Come where? Addie looked around her.

The window! She ran over to Paul Linn's window, which was cracked open. Mrs. Withers' room was next door, and her window must be open too. That was where the voices were coming from!

Oh, she gasped with relief, this is better and better. She kept one ear tuned to the conversation, and continued her search of Paul Linn's room. Her heart was pounding only slightly.

"Yes," Mrs. Withers was saying, "for once I've rather missed teaching these last few days. It would take my mind off things. All this waiting, waiting, and knowing that any moment the murderer could strike again!"

"Aren't you being rather melodramatic, Mrs. Withers?" came Paul Linn's voice in a careful, measured tone. Addie stopped short, her attention caught. Watch out, Mrs. Withers, thought Addie. She had heard that tone once before in class, when someone had taken Mr. Linn's top desk drawer and replaced it upside down. Mr. Linn's tone had been calm—conversational almost ("now, which of you is responsible for this, I wonder?") but with an undercurrent. And then—and then, thought Addie with a little thrill of remembrance, all hell had broken loose. Mr. Linn had shouted—Mr. Linn had thrown the contents of the drawer down the center aisle of desks—Mr. Linn's face had contorted with anger. When the storm had finally passed, there was absolute silence for the rest of the class hour. And no one, ever had dared to play a trick on Paul Linn again. Oh yes, Mrs. Withers, thought Addie, sitting on the windowsill, watch out!

"Why no, I don't think I'm being dramatic," Beatrice Withers was saying. "Why, Inspector Emery as much as said that whoever rifled Sarah's room is the murderer."

"He didn't, as a matter of fact, say that," said Paul, still tight and controlled. "You're being slightly ridiculous, Beatrice."

"Oh no, no, no," chanted Beatrice. "I don't think it's ridiculous at all. Of course, the inspector is mistaken. He thinks it's Alex. But *we* know that's not true. Don't we?"

Why, she knows, too, thought Addie. I wonder how she knows. But she's being awfully foolish.

"Just what are you getting at?" asked Paul. Can't she *tell*, thought Addie, can't she tell how much colder and colder that voice is getting . . . how cruel? Despite her curiosity, Addie had an almost overwhelming desire to give it all up, and run back as fast as she could to her own room, and slam the door, and be safe. . . .

"Oh, nothing," Beatrice chatted. "Remember how I told you the way I . . . notice things? I make a habit of it. I think people ought to cultivate their powers of observation. Like the way I noticed your room, remember? And how I mentioned there was nothing, you know, cozy and personal in it?"

Well, decided Addie, for once in her life Mrs.

Withers was right about something. There was nothing, absolutely nothing of any value in Paul Linn's room. Stacks of English texts, old exam papers, a pile of laundry, and a liquor stash. Very important clues, those. Addie sat down on the bed in disgust.

"They said that Lucie was the same way. They didn't find anything in her room to tell them who her family was, her friends, her . . . lovers. Just like you, Mr. Linn."

There was a harsh sound, a chair scraping perhaps.

"Only, you know, I found that odd. It seemed as though that simply couldn't be. Women save things, as I explained to you. And yet it had to be—the police couldn't have missed anything—they searched quite thoroughly. But there was one place they didn't search. One place they didn't even think about searching. I came across it quite by accident, just today. Lucie was awfully careless, leaving things about."

"What are you getting at?" said Paul again. There was a new element in his voice, which, Addie thought, might have been fear.

Mrs. Withers ignored the question. "So you've been seeing Melissa Willoughby. The rich Melissa Willoughby. Oh yes, Mr. Linn, you thought that was a secret, didn't you? Just goes to prove again how observant I am." She giggled. "Of course I suspected, but I wasn't *sure,* until today. Lucie wasn't very happy about that, was she? Not very happy at all.

"I have heard," she continued, "that Melissa

Willoughby is a terribly jealous woman. It seems to me that it would be awfully unpleasant, married to a jealous woman. I'm not the jealous sort, Mr. Linn. It's just not in me, I suppose, to be vicious and vindictive. Besides, you know. I understand men. And I understand that sometimes a man has to 'sow his wild oats' as the saying goes." The giggle again.

What an idiot that woman is, thought Addie. And why isn't Mr. Linn saying anything?

Finally he did speak. "What have you found, Beatrice?" And his voice was very quiet.

"A diary," she said, and her voice became quiet too, to match his own. "Her diary."

The silence became too heavy, almost, for Addie to bear. It seemed as though it would never be broken. She shivered, and wished Mrs. Withers would begin to chatter again. Addie had never thought she could be afraid of Mrs. Withers, but this new, quiet Mrs. Withers frightened her. She was talking again, in her new, quiet voice.

"I know you killed Lucie Jackson, and I know why. The diary doesn't, of course, prove that you killed her, since obviously she couldn't have known that beforehand."

"I did not, as a matter of fact, kill her," said Paul tightly.

"Oh, I may not be able to prove it, but it doesn't matter. Even aside from the idea of murder, if Melissa Willoughby should have any idea that you were involved with Lucie, well . . ."

"And just what are you going to do?"

"Well, there are three alternatives. One, I could go to Melissa, in which case, there would go your fortune. Two, I could go to the police. They'd think I was a silly hysterical woman, of course, but it would start them thinking. . . ."

"And three?"

"Three, I don't say anything to anybody."

There was a silence.

"I won't, you know . . . Paul . . . say anything, that is. I wanted to let you know that. But I've kept the diary in quite a safe place—I see you looking around—it's not here. Don't get the idea I'd give it to you. But its existence—that can be our little secret."

Another silence. Addie felt her skin prickle and her stomach twist with nervousness. Any moment Paul Linn could lose his temper, and storm out of the room . . . and into his own. But she had to hear . . . she just had to.

"I wouldn't even mind if you did marry Melissa," said Beatrice. "I told a white lie earlier —I am a tiny bit jealous. I was jealous of Lucie —but I'm not jealous of Melissa Willoughby. No, I wouldn't even mind if you did marry her. Just long enough to get some of that money you want so much. Just as long as you didn't *stay* married to her. I'm in no hurry."

"No hurry for what?" said the tight voice.

"No hurry," she said, "to be your wife." And Addie could tell by her voice that she was smiling.

Chapter Eleven

It was only Paul Linn's famous temper which saved Addie. He stormed out of Beatrice's room before Addie had a chance to escape, but instead of returning to his own room, he took the stairs two at a time and burst out the front door. Paul's cure for anger was to drive his car like a maniac through the back roads of town, and he strode down the driveway toward the garage. From his window Addie could see him, and in a few moments the car drove away.

Addie waited until her pulse had returned to some semblance of normal before she left Paul's room and returned to her own. Her hand was shaking as she found Harrison's home number and dialed it.

"Uncle H," her voice came over the phone in an urgent whisper. "I've got something vitally important to tell you. . . ."

Harrison's expression changed as he listened. "I see," he said. "Yes. You're sure? *You* saw

Paul Linn last night from your window? No, you were right to call me. Anything else?"

He listened a few more moments, and straightened up with an enraged expression on his face. "Addie!" his voice rose. "Didn't I tell you to keep out of this? Not to go snooping around? And the very first thing you do . . . Mrs. Withers? . . . Are you sure?"

Matthew had come out from the kitchen into the hall. He looked surprised and curious. Harrison attempted to compose himself. "No, I suppose not," he said in a quieter voice. "All right. I'll be over right away. What kind of car does Paul Linn drive, do you know? . . . All right. Don't say anything to anyone about this. And stay out of trouble! Don't do anything! Stay in your room! Read! Take a nap!" He hung up the phone, shaking his head.

"Now what the heck," said Matt, "was that all about?"

Harrison seemed not to have heard him. He hesitated a moment, then made a call to his office and ordered a search be made for a man driving a small red sportscar. Mr. Linn wasn't to be arrested, just followed. Harrison made one or two other requests, then hung up.

Shortly after, when Harrison arrived at Mrs. Otto's school and turned the corner to pull into the driveway, Addie was there to meet him. He sighed. He stopped the car at the corner, out of sight of the house, and got out.

"Mr. Linn's not back yet," announced Addie. "Mrs. Otto is in the drawing room. And Mrs.

Withers hasn't come out of her room. I thought you'd never get here. Are you going to arrest Mrs. Withers?"

"It depends on what I find in her room. If she *does* have a diary of Lucie Jackson's, then she's been withholding evidence. . . ."

"Oh, you won't find it in her room. She told Mr. Linn she didn't have it there. And besides, I already . . ." She broke off abruptly, and began to study a piece of tree-bark with elaborate interest.

"You already—oh, no." Harrison put a hand to his forehead and closed his eyes. "You don't mean you searched Paul Linn's room and then you searched Beatrice Withers' room *too*?"

"No," said Addie. "Actually I searched Mrs. Withers' room and *then* I searched Mr. Linn's room. I searched Mrs. Withers' room yesterday, in fact. I had to, you see. Gwyneth and Phyllis saw her. They saw her coming in from the garden and she was looking furtive. So of course I had to find out why."

"She was looking what?"

"Furtive. She was carrying something and hoping no one would see her. It must have been the diary. She must have taken it up to her room and read it and then hidden it somewhere."

"Do you have any idea where?"

"No, but then I really haven't had time to think. It never dawned on me she might have something important until I heard her talking." Addie glanced up, in the direction of the house, and shivered slightly. "You'd better go on up to the house now. Mrs. Otto might have seen your car by now. Mrs. Otto sees everything. She won't like it if she finds out that I've been out here talking to you without her knowing it. She won't like it that I called you. But I guess there's no way of getting around that, is there? She'll have to know. . . ."

"I expect she will. Well, I'd better be going."

"Me, too. I'll go around the back way. See you later!" Addie scampered off, her hair flying.

"I don't know anything about a diary. I don't know what you're talking about, Inspector," said Beatrice Withers. "Harassing me, badgering me . . ."

"For heaven's sake, Beatrice, nobody's badgering you," said Mrs. Otto. "Inspector, that sounds very much like the notebook I told you I'd seen Lucinda writing in. But you said yourself your men searched everything thoroughly, the entire house, including Beatrice's room. How could she have found something they missed?" Mrs. Otto's tone was quite accusatory.

"How indeed?" echoed Beatrice Withers triumphantly. "Go ahead, search my room if you like. Go ahead! You won't find any diary. You won't find anything there!"

"I know," said Harrison. He groaned inwardly. He had been gambling on Beatrice breaking down at the mention of the diary—she had surprised him. There was only one course left to him.

"Mrs. Otto, would you ask my niece to come downstairs, please?"

"Adelaide?" Mrs. Otto's surprise was evident. Beatrice looked up, furious. "That scheming, sneaking little devil?" she said. "Has she been telling you stories about me? The lying little . . ."

"Beatrice," said Mrs. Otto, "that is Mr. Emery's niece you are referring to. Please refrain from making insulting remarks. Sarah!" Sarah appeared, looking apprehensive. "Bring Adelaide in here, please."

A few moments later, Addie entered the room. Harrison noted the addition, since he had met her at the gate, of a wide yellow hair ribbon. She looked very innocent. She sat down in a big armchair without a word and crossed her ankles daintily. Beatrice Withers fixed a savage glare upon her, which Addie ignored.

Harrison cleared his throat. "Mrs. Otto, Addie called me earlier this morning and told me some things which I thought ought to be checked out. She's been—ah—snooping a bit, I'm afraid. I know that what she did was wrong, and I am not trying to condone it—but I hope you won't be too hard on her." (Addie managed to look more innocent than ever.) "She was only trying to help, and it's quite important, from the standpoint of the case, that she saw and heard what she did."

"Or what she says she saw!" snarled Beatrice. "The sneaking little . . ."

Mrs. Otto turned to Addie. "Go ahead,

Adelaide," she said, without the hint of any emotion in her voice. "Tell us what you saw."

"I didn't actually 'see' anything," Addie began, "but I certainly did hear a lot." Beatrice blinked. "I heard Mrs. Withers tell Mr. Linn that she had found a diary that belonged to Miss Jackson—and that she knew from what it said that Mr. Linn was the murderer."

"How absurd!" said Beatrice. But Harrison noted with satisfaction that she had turned pale.

Addie took a deep breath. "And of course Mr. Linn got very mad and wanted her to give him the diary but she said she didn't have it—that she'd put it somewhere he'd never find it. And she said not to worry—she wouldn't tell anyone, or give him away—if he would marry her.

"Well, it's true," said Addie as she felt Mrs. Otto's disbelieving eyes upon her. "I'm only saying what happened."

Beatrice sputtered. "Mrs. Otto, surely you are not going to take the word of this lying child . . . why, as if I would . . ."

But Mrs. Otto was not paying any attention to Beatrice Withers. She turned to Harrison. "It really doesn't matter, does it, Inspector, whether I —or you—believe this story? As I said before, if a diary cannot be produced, your charges against Mrs. Withers are meaningless."

Beatrice Withers smirked.

"Addie?" said Harrison. "Are you sure you didn't hear anything that might give you a clue as to where this diary is?"

"This 'alleged' diary," put in Beatrice

Withers. She put her nose into the air. "There is no such thing. I would like this child punished—punished se-vere-ly, for what she has dared to accuse me of. The very idea, why, I never, never in all my life, never in all my life . . ."

Addie snapped her fingers. "I've got it!"

They all looked at her. "I just this minute got it! I *do* know where Mrs. Withers hid that diary. I knew it would come to me. But not from anything she said to Mr. Linn. I just now remembered." She jumped up excitedly.

"Remember, Uncle Harrison, I was telling you about that first day when you were questioning Mrs. Withers out in the garden? And I told you we just happened to be looking out our window at the time? And that later on Phyllis and Gwyneth just happened to see Mrs. Withers come back from the garden carrying something —the diary, of course—and looking furtive?"

"Yes, you told me about all the things you just happened to see."

"Well, I'll bet I know where she was bringing it back from. Not the garden, but the greenhouse. And I'll bet, after she read it, that she put it right back there. In the greenhouse. No one would think of looking there."

"The greenhouse? Why the greenhouse?"

"Because," said Addie, "it all fits. Miss Jackson used to go out there to practice her lines for plays and things. She said she could think better out there—and that the sound was good, too. Mrs. Withers was out there digging around with spades and things. She'd have had to take them back to the greenhouse and put them away—that's where the tools were kept."

"We didn't search the greenhouse," said Harrison slowly.

Beatrice Withers, unexpectedly, began to howl. She cried and cried hysterically, digging unsuccessfully into her bag for a handkerchief. "It's true, oh, it's true. I never should have done it, but I thought ... oh, I thought ... ohhhhh. . . . . ."

"Pull yourself together, Mrs. Withers," said Harrison. The stern tone of his voice, oddly enough, quieted her. She sniffled loudly, finally produced the sought-for handkerchief, and blew her nose. "I'll show you where it is now if you like," she said in a small voice.

"That would be very kind of you."

The air was chilly as they walked out to the greenhouse, and the clouds hovered close, threatening a storm. They did not speak. Beatrice Withers cried all the way out to the greenhouse.

"It's kind of eerie out here," whispered Addie to Harrison. They had dropped a little behind Mrs. Otto and Beatrice, and Mrs. Otto occasionally turned around to look back. "I never liked it out in the greenhouse. It gives me claustrophobia or something, every time I go in here. Like I want to get away as quick as I can. Like one of those vines could just reach out and grab you."

"Thanks," said Harrison. They reached the threshold. The air which wafted out as they opened the door was clammy. Harrison, too, felt a wave of distate flow over him. Addie suddenly took hold of his hand.

The greenhouse was a larger one than most, and had a front and back door. Flowers and plants were everywhere, some of them almost unhealthily oversized. And Addie was right: whoever chose the greenery (Alex? Mrs. Otto?) had a penchant for long and clinging vines.

"Here it is," sobbed Beatrice. They came to a small plaster bench, nearly surrounded and hidden by plants. Beatrice reached down behind the bench and pulled out a small black rectangle.

"How did you find this? Is this where it was hidden originally?" Harrison took the package from her.

"Yes. I just came out here—it was right after you questioned me. I don't know why I came out here exactly, I was thinking about Lucie, I guess. Anyway, I came here and sat down. And I dropped my necklace. While I was reaching down behind the bench to pick it up, I felt something. It was her diary. I was so scared I didn't know what to do—I didn't dare read it right then—Alex might have come in. And besides, Inspector, you were still here. So I quickly hurried back to my own room with it, and read it there."

"And didn't say a word to anyone about it," said Harrison.

Beatrice started to sniffle again. "I meant to. I

truly meant to. But then I thought, well, maybe not just yet. Paul didn't *mean* to kill her. I'm sure of that. She must have provoked him into it. You don't know what she was like, Inspector. I know it wasn't really Paul's fault."

"So you were going to blackmail him into marrying you. Weren't you afraid of marrying a man who was a murderer?"

"Why no. I've just told you. It wasn't his fault. She probably provoked him. Poor Paul does have an awful temper."

Addie looked up. "He seemed to be in a pretty bad temper with you earlier, Mrs. Withers, when you told him about the diary," she pointed out. "He seemed pretty provoked then." Beatrice Withers opened her mouth, then shut it again without speaking.

"Well, Inspector," said Mrs. Otto, "I suppose this proves beyond all doubt that Paul Linn is the murderer."

"I haven't read the diary yet, Mrs. Otto, I don't know. I don't see, really, how it could. Lucie didn't know, after all, that she was about to be murdered. How could she have written about it?"

"But the book talks all about her affair with Mr. Linn," said Beatrice Withers. Now that her secret was out, she wanted to be the first one to break the news. "And you know he did deny that."

Harrison took the black, leather-bound notebook and turned it over in his hands. He opened it, randomly, somewhere near the middle.

Lucie Jackson's handwriting was as he would have expected from descriptions of her personality: large capital letters, dramatic flourishes. The words were hurried, even sloppy, with ink smudges riddling the pages, as if the words could not be written down fast enough to suit her thoughts. The sentences themselves were choppy, and often not finished.

The book did seem, as Mrs. Otto had mentioned, to be concerned mainly with drama notes —ideas for stage sets and character portrayals, things like that. But Harrison's eyes fell upon one paragraph that was different.

The paragraph read: "It's nearly time for the final act. I suppose I am, really, the villain in my own private play. How funny."

That was all.

Beatrice Withers was looking over the Inspector's shoulder. "It says things like that all through the whole book. Just here and there. Half the time I didn't have any idea what she meant by the things she said. Don't you think that's odd?"

A picture brushed through Harrison's mind, suddenly. Though he had never met the murdered woman, he seemed to see her face before him. She was laughing, and it was not a pleasant laugh. Taunting him. "She was always saying things she thought we wouldn't understand," Addie had said. "And then wouldn't explain what she meant."

The picture was too real. He shut the diary

abruptly. "I'll take this back to my office to study it."

Harrison suddenly, very badly, wanted to be out of this place. Something in the glass that roofed the greenhouse made everyone's skin look a pale, yellowish gray. How could Alex bear to spend time in a place like this? And what of Lucie Jackson, who chose to spend her solitary hours here?

"What about . . . what about Mr. Linn?" ventured Beatrice.

"I have a feeling," said Harrison, "that Mr. Linn is not going to be around this afternoon. However, I have a car out looking for him. If he does return, Mrs. Otto, I'd appreciate it if you'd tell him for me that he'd better not leave again. I'm going to need to talk to him. And I want to find him here when I do."

He opened the door and led them out of the greenhouse. The fresh chill air of the outdoors felt wonderful. He turned to Mrs. Otto. "I'll be leaving now. I'm going back to the station and check out this diary—and a few other things. I'll get back to you. And don't hesitate to call if you need me."

"Inspector," said Mrs. Otto sternly. "Are you going to let Paul Linn stay here, until you need him? Free? A killer?"

"We don't know if he's a killer," said Harrison. "We don't know that yet. And don't worry—we're going to be keeping a very close eye on Paul Linn. You won't need to worry."

"I wish," said Mrs. Otto, "that I shared your confidence on that score." But somehow her tone was not as icy as it was meant to be. She put a hand to her hair, caught Addie watching her and dropped it back down to her side. The gesture reminded Harrison of something, but he couldn't quite put his finger on what it was. Perhaps it would come.

"I'll be going now," he said. "And Addie," he put a hand on her shoulder, "I *think* I can handle things from now on, all right? No more of this 'just happened to see something,' all right?"

"All right," said Addie, subdued.

"Please don't be too hard on her, Mrs. Otto," said Harrison. "I'm sure she won't interfere again. And after all, she did lead us to the diary. I might not have found it without her help."

Mrs. Otto gave him a thin smile. "Good day, Inspector." With one last apprehensive glance at Addie, Harrison turned and left.

When he had gone, Mrs. Otto turned to Addie with an unreadable expression on her face. "So, you knew where Lucie Jackson's diary was. I wonder what else you know."

Addie didn't say a word, but raised her chin a fraction of an inch, and gazed at Mrs. Otto. Though she came not quite to Mrs. Otto's shoulder, the strange battle of wills was an evenly matched one. They looked at each other for not quite a minute.

Then a twig snapped—disturbing the silence. Mrs. Otto looked away. "Come," she said. "It's time we went back to the house."

Chapter Twelve

Addie and Mrs. Otto had walked in silence back to the house from the greenhouse. Addie had gone straight to her room where Gwyneth and Phyllis, dancing with impatience, had met her.

"Weren't you scared, Addie?" asked Phyllis when she had heard. "Weren't you just scared to death? When Mrs. Withers said you were lying? And Mrs. Otto said 'tell us what you know, Adelaide? Oh, it just makes my blood run cold!'"

"And after all that spying and everything," marveled Gwyneth, "Mrs. Otto didn't even punish you."

"Not yet, anyway," said Addie. "Maybe she's thinking up something really extra special."

Addie was glad to be back in her room. So much had happened in the space of one afternoon. So much to think about, and sort out. . . .

"Did you get to read any of the diary?" asked Phyllis.

"No, darn it. But Mrs. Withers said it told that Miss Jackson was awfully jealous of a rich lady that Mr. Linn is planning to marry. A Melissa Willoughby."

"I didn't know *that*! Mr. Linn—getting married!"

"Nobody knew. I think that was just the point. From what I can make out, Mr. Linn was trying to keep it a secret. He was also trying to keep his affair with Miss Jackson a secret from Melissa Willoughby, because *she* was jealous too and might not have married him if she knew. Then he wouldn't have gotten any of her money, which is the only reason he wanted to marry her in the first place.

"So Miss Jackson was trying to get back at him by blackmailing him. She said, I guess, that she'd tell Melissa Willoughby *everything* unless he gave her money.

"Mrs. Withers thinks that Mr. Linn got so mad at Miss Jackson—'provoked' is what she said—that he killed her in a fit of anger. Got so furious with her demands and her threats and things, that he just couldn't stand it any more."

"Well," said Gwyneth, "that's logical."

"No," said Addie. "No, it isn't." She walked to the window and drew open the curtains. She looked out across the garden, to the roof of the greenhouse, then up to the overcast sky. She turned back around, frowning.

"Miss Jackson was strangled in her sleep. That means that the killer *planned* to do it. I can believe that Mr. Linn would have gotten angry enough to kill Miss Jackson, but he would have done it right *then,* at the height of his anger, right in the middle of an argument or something. He wouldn't have planned ahead to kill her . . . he wouldn't have waited until she was asleep."

Addie looked back through the window. "So many things," she said, almost to herself. "Little things that don't fit. That don't seem important. Little things that somebody maybe saw, or heard, or knows. A little thing that might turn out to be important."

"But Addie, you said it was Mr. Linn for sure." Phyllis tugged at her hair with her usual gesture of nervousness. "The Ouija board said it was him. It must be him."

Addie moved away from the window and looked hard at Phyllis. "I thought you liked Mr. Linn."

"I do. Oh, I do. I like him better than almost anyone!"

"Well, then . . ."

"Well, nothing," snapped Gwyneth. "You just want to be right, that's all. You said it was Mr. Linn and now you're worried you might be wrong, so however it turns out you're going to make it seem like you knew all along."

Addie ignored Gwyneth. "Phyllis, *did* you see something that night? Something that might prove it was Mr. Linn? Or something that might prove it wasn't? You said you were asleep. Do you know something you haven't told us?"

"No . . . oh no!" Phyllis pulled hard on a lock of hair. So hard that it must have hurt.

Chapter Thirteen

"What are you muttering about over there, Harrison?" Sergeant Jeff Willes looked up from his desk.

"What?"

"Muttering," Jeff repeated patiently. "You're muttering. Talking about villains, and plays, and all kinds of strange stuff. Are you still working on that diary?"

It was later that afternoon, nearly four o'clock. Harrison had just received a call telling him that Paul Linn had been found, driving his car on a country road some ten miles from town. He had been given a speeding ticket and advised to return to the school—that he could expect to be questioned further on the subject of his involvement with the murder victim. That meant another trip out to the school on top of the one Harrison had just made, and he did not relish the idea. The afternoon was getting darker and grayer, foreshadowing another storm, and Harrison wished he had nothing more on his mind than going home, drinking cocoa in front of the fire and reading *The Life and Times of Winston Churchill*—and possibly nodding off to a late-afternoon nap.

Instead, he was working late, concentrating on the confused, cryptic diary of a murdered woman.

"If I could only put it all together," Harrison muttered. "The whole diary is full of clues, if I could just figure them out. I can just imagine Lucie Jackson looking over my shoulder, taunting me, saying 'but it's so obvious, you fool.' That's what Addie said about her, that she enjoyed being mysterious and secretive. But what was her secret? Whatever it was, she was murdered for it." He got up from his desk and began to pace. Jeff Willes, unable to concentrate on the report he was preparing, gave up and turned his full attention to Harrison's mutterings.

"Just suppose," said Harrison, looking up at the clock, "that two things tie in: the line in the diary about Lucie being the villain in her own play, and the remark she made to her host at the New Year's party. She was going to do something evil, and she was going to enjoy it. The 'something evil' probably was blackmail. She was going to threaten, or demand money from someone, that very night. . . ."

"From Paul Linn, of course," Jeff put in. He walked over to Harrison's desk. "I read that diary too. It's perfectly clear she was blackmailing Paul. Look, it says right here. . ." he flipped though pages " '. . . he'll be sorry. Leaving me for that witch, just because she's rich and I'm poor. Well, I'll never be poor again.' Isn't that obvious? She was going to blackmail him to get back at him. Blackmail him out of his rich fiancee's money—it's just the kind of ironic touch that would have appealed to her, don't you think?"

"By the way," said Willes, "I've met the charming fiancee. Checked with her earlier this afternoon, trying to locate Linn. She's going to sue for false arrest, *and* she's going to make sure I lose my job. Do I *know* who her father *is?* she asks. How dare I accuse her Paul of anything, she asks!"

Harrison laughed. "Oh yes, she's a charmer, all right." He paced again. "All right, I'm willing to admit that Lucie was blackmailing Paul. But I can't shake the feeling that some of the sentences in this book were not meant to refer to Paul. Supposing he wasn't the only one she was blackmailing? Look, that sentence you just read for instance: 'I'll never be poor again.' It's on the next page, the right-hand page. Supposing there was a page torn out in between. So that the 'I'll never be poor again' line refers not to Paul but to someone, or something, else!"

"I've lost you," said Willes.

"I know it's far-fetched. But look, this is one of those spiral-type notebooks with the pages easily torn out. There are supposed to be 150 sheets, but I've counted and there are only 143.

What's happened to the other seven?"

"She probably just tore them out, you know, made a mistake and threw them away."

"Suppose someone else tore those pages out? Look, Lucie's made mistakes all the way through the book, and she certainly didn't bother to throw those pages out. Look at this page, for instance. She spilled ink all over it. And this page, it's all scribbled out. Why didn't she tear those out?" Harrison began riffling through pages. "And, if I'm right and someone else did tear out those seven pages, it certainly wasn't Paul. He wouldn't have left in pages that incriminated him so obviously.

"Here's another page. Here on the left side it reads, 'He'll be sorry. How I hate him. He'll be sorry—I'll bet he's sorry already.' Then here, on the right-hand page: 'Controlling people—what a sense of power it brings. And it's so easy!' Now I don't know what that means, but it doesn't really seem to fit what was on the page before. It doesn't seem to refer specifically to Paul, the way the first part does. It says 'controlling people,' plural."

"Don't you think you're grasping at straws, Harrison? I think you just don't want it to be Paul."

Harrison smiled ruefully. "You're probably right. I have to admit I don't want it to be him. I like the man, damn it. He's obviously a liar, and a skunk, and a fortune-hunter—but he's likeable. Besides," he tried again, "it just doesn't fit. Something's wrong somewhere." He began to pace about the room again. Jeff Willes felt slightly dizzy trying to follow his movements, as well as his thoughts.

"Paul Linn's not stupid," said Harrison, "and he's charming, very charming to women. Granted, heiresses aren't exactly a dime a dozen, but they're not extinct either. If Melissa threw him over, he could find someone else. His whole life didn't depend on Melissa. So the money motive isn't strong enough."

Harrison stared out the window to the steadily darkening afternoon sky. "And what about love?"

"Love?"

"The hero finally finds the woman he loves, only to have an evil woman from out of his past emerge and threaten to blow the whole thing. Even when Bette Davis plays it, you don't quite believe it. But Melissa Willoughby? Somehow I just can't visualize Paul Linn not being able to bear life without his beloved Melissa. You've met her. Can you?"

Jeff Willes laughed shortly and shrugged his shoulders. "No, I sure can't."

"No," said Harrison, "Paul Linn's motive is just not strong enough. Not unless there's a lot more I don't know."

"And what's his story? Paul Linn's, I mean?"

"Well, I don't know yet. I haven't talked to him. He doesn't know I've found the diary—unless someone at the school has told him, that is.

I'll be interested to see whether he persists in denying his relationship with Lucie. I'm on my way out there now to talk to him."

"Well," said Willes sagely (in the manner of one who has watched too many detective movies) "I just hope you don't let him slip through your fingers. Slippery weasel, if you ask me. If you ask me, anybody who tries to mix a jealous mistress with a jealous fiancee deserves whatever he gets!"

Harrison picked up his raincoat, then turned back with an afterthought. "Just suppose, for the sake of argument, that I'm right. That Lucie was blackmailing someone besides Paul, and that other person was the one she intended to see —the reason she left the party early.

"Now, let's just assume this is what happened: Lucie comes back to the school. Either on the way back from the party, or later, after saying goodnight to Beatrice and Mrs. Otto, she speaks to that person, threatens him possibly. That person, Mr. or Ms. X, does nothing at the time, but later, after Lucie is asleep, comes back into her room and strangles her.

"She probably didn't have time to stop along the way home from the party. So that points to someone in the house. Someone she talked to after saying goodnight to Beatrice and Mrs. Otto —after she supposedly went to bed."

"Someone in the house? But who? Alex?"

"Possibly. I checked up on him. He served some time for theft a few years ago—hence his hatred of police, I suppose. Mrs. Otto certainly wouldn't have hired him if she'd known that. Lucie might have found that out, and threatened to use it against him."

"And you did say Sarah Bow was acting suspiciously about him."

"As if she were trying to protect him. She certainly didn't want to admit that that pin was his. She might have known his secret too. But it's still pretty thin."

"Who else besides Alex? Are you sure the motive has to be blackmail? I can't imagine Mrs. Otto, the paragon, having any dark secrets. And Beatrice Withers is too dull to have any. But," said Jeff, "Beatrice might have had another motive—jealousy. Maybe she was so jealous of Paul and Lucie that she killed her to get her out of the way."

"Yes, Mrs. Withers," said Harrison thoughtfully. "There's more to her than I had thought. She's not quite the scatterbrain she seems. And it's obvious she hated Lucie. Viciously. I think envy is precisely the reason for that hatred. But," said Harrison, "there's no money involved in that reason. Lucie talked so much about acquiring money soon, that I can't think it was coincidence. I'm sure that had something to do with her being murdered. Money—and blackmail."

"Well, I'm putting my money on Paul Linn," said Willes. "You just try to make things hard for yourself, Harrison. You know you do." And

Jeff Willes turned back to his report.

On the way out to his car, the bits and pieces of Lucie's diary collided against each other in his mind. Again, he felt her taunting him. But it was not Harrison she had intended to taunt, it was someone else.

Harrison, who did not like cats, was suddenly reminded of Matthew's cat. He had watched it one day taunting a mouse it had caught, letting it run a bit, almost escape, then draw it back into its clutches. A bird had flown by, not seeing the cat, and had landed in a nearby bush. The cat had abandoned the nearly-dead mouse, to stalk the bird. Greedy, it wanted both. With that image, superimposed upon the image of Lucie's laughing face, came an odd surge of sympathy for her killer. Who could blame the mouse for killing the cat, if only it could?

Chapter Fourteen

When Harrison turned the corner to enter the gate to Mrs. Otto's School to question Paul Linn, a big, silver Jaguar sat squarely in the way. There was no way of getting around it. Harrison sighed irritably as he parked by the side of the road and began walking the quarter-mile drive up to the school.

A car like that, in this town, could belong to only one person: Jacob Willoughby. Harrison surmised that Melissa Willoughby had come to pay a visit.

And so she had. When Harrison entered the drawing room, his attention was immediately drawn to a red-clad figure sitting squarely in the middle of the sofa, thin legs crossed haughtily, smoking a cigarette from a holder. Melissa Willoughby was dressed in what was supposed to be the latest—and most expensive—word in fashion. ('Vermilion for boldness,' cried the fashion magazines, 'a hint of not-quite-pink for softness—not simply an outfit, but a creation!') A large mushroom in the same awful red as the dress perched atop her head, and a red ostrich feather protruded from it. Harrison, being ignorant of the nuances of fashion, thought she looked exactly like a lobster. The effect was heightened by clawlike fingernails.

Beatrice Withers sat at the piano bench, a black glare fixed on the back of Melissa's head as though to put a hex on her. Paul Linn lolled against the mantel. Mrs. Otto rose from her straight-backed armchair to greet Harrison.

"Miss Willoughby, this is Inspector Harrison Emery," said Mrs. Otto with chilly poise. "Inspector Emery, Miss Melissa Willoughby."

Melissa Willoughby's reputation for unpleasantness was well-founded. "I know who he is," she snapped. "What I want to know is what he thinks he's doing.

"I thought," she said icily, "that the murderer had been found. I thought it was perfectly clear who the murderer is. That gardener person. And yet . . . and yet," and her voice grew shrill, "one of your 'men' " (she spat out the word) "follows my Paul and insinuates that he has something to do with all this! The very idea! I've never been so insulted in my life!"

Paul Linn exploded. "And just what the hell do you think you're doing here? I can handle my own affairs, thank you. I don't need you running over here on my behalf."

"Well, you don't seem to be doing a particularly good job of handling them so far," retorted

Melissa. "Getting yourself mixed up in murder, indeed."

Harrison's eyes flicked to Beatrice Withers, who was obviously enjoying this interchange.

Mrs. Otto interrupted. "As you may have gathered, Inspector, no one has said anything to Mr. Linn or Miss Willoughby about the—latest development in the case. We thought it better to wait for you."

"What latest development?" snapped Melissa. Beatrice Withers smiled.

"I think, Mr. Linn, it might be better if you and I spoke alone."

When they were alone (Melissa having swept off in a fury), Harrison told Paul about Addie's eavesdropping in his room, and about the finding of the diary. There was a silence, then an unexpected reaction. Paul Linn exploded with laughter.

"That little beast! I might have expected something like that from her. Well, she's got guts anyway, I must admit that. So she heard the whole thing from beginning to end?"

"More or less. She said if you'd gone back into your room instead of down the stairs, you'd have caught her red-handed."

"Hah! I wish I had." Paul laughed again, and shook his head. "What a scene that would have been! What would poor old Beatrice have done then? Her blackmail scheme foiled by a 13-year-old girl." Paul seemed remarkably cheerful, thought Harrison, considering that he had just been accused of murder.

"Well, Inspector, I don't mind telling you, I'm a bit relieved you've found me out. All these secrets. And today, Beatrice, that about took the cake. As if she'd think I'd marry her! She's a crazy old bat. All the same, that melodrama. And she really acted as though she knew something. Made me wonder for a minute if I really was the murderer! Strike that last part," he grinned. "Don't write that down.

"All right," he said, lighting up a cigarette. "I had an affair with Lucie. It was all good sport. She said so too, playing the emancipated woman. It was all a game, she didn't care a thing about me either, just wanted to have a good time, and so on. Fool that I was, I took her at her word.

"I was making a play for Melissa at the time, too. I mean, I figured, why not? Lucie and I had everything straight between us, right? Hah! But when Lucie began to sense that I was getting away from her—well, then! Exit the emancipated woman, enter the wronged damsel in distress. What an act she put on! Threatening to go to Melissa. I didn't take her too seriously—gave her a few trinkets. It seemed to pacify her. I never dreamed she was keeping a diary. I was careful not to write her any letters, and I thought she had been too. You could have knocked me over with a feather when I heard Mrs. Otto say she'd been keeping a diary.

"That's why I tried Sarah's room. I'd searched

everywhere else I could think of. Because if you did find it, you'd know I lied, even if I tried to squeeze out of it."

Harrison looked at Paul steadily. "You're sure she wasn't trying to seriously blackmail you?"

There was a short silence, in which the atmosphere almost imperceptibly changed. Paul Linn, thought Harrison, was worried. "She was beginning to," he said finally, soberly. "Damn her, she was beginning to. I should have known she wouldn't be satisfied with trinkets. She was greedy. She was putting the screws to me. If Melissa hadn't been as jealous as she was . . . listen, Inspector, I was just trying to satisfy Lucie. I was borrowing money from Melissa, who didn't care, not knowing what it was for, of course. But I wouldn't have let it go too far. You've got to believe that. Marrying Melissa wasn't that important to me. I wouldn't have killed for her money."

Paul took a deep breath and continued. "Oh, I wanted it, wanted it badly. I admit that. I've got a taste for the good life and I'm tired of wasting time in this out-of-the-way place. Mrs. Otto may make good money from all those gullible well-heeled parents, but she sure doesn't pass much of it on to us. I'm tired of things the way they are. I want out. But I didn't want out that badly. I wasn't going to let Lucie bully me. I was going to call it all to a halt. I was going to tell Lucie she could tell Melissa anything she liked. You've got to believe me—I was going to!"

Chapter Fifteen

The sky had been turning grayer and grayer all afternoon, and as Harrison walked outside the house and down the path toward his car, he thought he felt a drop of rain. He shivered and walked faster. Just great, he thought. Because of Melissa Willoughby and her haughty Jaguar, he was going to get soaked.

"Uncle Harrison!" Addie ran toward him, neatly dressed in a trim trench coat and matching hat. She even looked like a spy, a miniature one. Harrison was irritable.

"What are you doing here? Didn't I tell you to stop spying?"

"I haven't been spying," she said in an injured tone. "But I . . . well, I have a feeling. A very strong feeling.

"It's Phyllis," she said. "I haven't paid enough attention to Phyllis. What I mean is, Phyllis is just kind of *there*, in the background— she never says much. But she was there that night—the night of the murder—and she saw something. I know it."

"You know it? She told you?"

"No, and that's what so strange. Phyllis can't keep a secret. Usually I can pry anything out of her I want to. But not this time. It never occurred to me to try, at first. I mean, what could she know? Things always occur to me, always," Addie said sadly. "But not this time. Not till just a little while ago."

"Listen, Addie, in about two minutes it's going to start pouring rain and I'm going to get soaked. *And* I'm in a hurry. You mean you think she saw something the night of the murder that might be important? We questioned her already, and she was sound asleep at the time."

"She says she was asleep. You did just like I did, you didn't even think that she might know something. But I'm afraid if you question her now, she still won't tell you what she knows. She's scared, scared of—something. Besides, she'd get into trouble because she knew something and didn't come forward before. Phyllis is awfully afraid of getting into trouble."

"Why did you come out here to tell me all this?" asked Harrison, not sure he wanted to hear the answer.

"I have something in mind. Another Ouija board session." Quickly Addie sketched in the previous Ouija board session, which had incriminated Paul Linn.

"And it looks as though the Ouija might be right, too. All the evidence points to him. But still . . . I mean, I right away suspected him. I'd heard conversations between him and Miss Jackson—I'd suspected that they were lovers. And I logically deduced that he was the murderer. I'd had my mind pretty much made up, even before we asked the Ouija.

"The thing with the Ouija board," said Addie seriously, "is that I don't, I really don't, move the board. Gwyneth accuses me of it, but I don't. But I know that sometimes when I think something, the Ouija board spells it out. It's not some spirit, it's *me*. Even though I don't do it on purpose, and even though the Ouija sometimes puts things differently—still, the ideas are mine. Especially," she said, "when I do it with Phyllis. I have a theory about that. I think that my personality is so much stronger than hers that her thoughts don't influence the Ouija board at all— and so mine come through loud and clear.

"My theory is this," continued Addie. "Phyllis believes completely in the Ouija board. She thinks everything it says is true—everything. Even if it talks nonsense, which it does sometimes. So Phyllis believes Paul Linn is the murderer, absolutely, because the Ouija board told her so."

It was definitely beginning to rain. Harrison shifted impatiently.

"So," said Addie, "if Phyllis saw the real murderer that night, and it wasn't Mr. Linn, and if for some reason she didn't want to admit it, she'd think it couldn't possibly matter whether she said anything or not, because it would have no bearing on the case anyway. Paul Linn is the murderer, period—in her mind."

"Addie. . ."

"Now what I want to do is have another Ouija session, with Phyllis and me working the board, in which the Ouija board says that it was wrong, and that Mr. Linn isn't guilty—which isn't going to be easy to do, because the Ouija hates to admit being wrong—but somehow. Then, if the Ouija were to say that Miss Jackson's ghost is angry because her murder hasn't been avenged, and that she is angry with Phyllis, why then, we could pry it out of her easily. That would scare her more than anything else."

That got Harrison's full attention. He had been irritable, now he was angry. Addie, seeing his face, rushed on. "I know what you're going to say. I know it's mean to scare her—but it's the only way I can think of. Uncle Harrison, if I haven't been able to figure out what she knows, then nothing can, except this. And I would bet you anything in the world that she knows something, something important. I know it."

"Just for the record," said Harrison, "why did you come here to tell me this? You know perfectly well I won't approve a scheme like this."

"Because," said Addie with deadly seriousness, "it scares me. I have a feeling that I shouldn't do it, and yet I have to do it. I have a feeling that if I do, something bad is going to happen."

The sky suddenly seemed darker, more foreboding. "That's why I want you to be there," said Addie. "That is, not there exactly, not with us, but just—nearby. Couldn't you arrange to come out this evening? On some pretext? I don't want to take any chances."

"You're not going to take any chances, Addie. I forbid, do you hear, I forbid you to monkey around with something like this. You've gotten into enough trouble already. You persist," said Harrison, his voice rising, "in treating this as some kind of game. This is dangerous. I've tried to tell you that before. A woman has been murdered. Dangerous!"

"I knew you would say that," she sulked. "I've helped so far, haven't I? I've found out just as much as you have. It seems to me you ought to listen to me more. Even if I am just a child."

"I don't want you getting hurt. And I don't want you scaring Phyllis." Harrison calmed down slightly. "I'll tell you what. I've got some things to do this evening, but tomorrow morning first thing I'll come out and talk to Phyllis privately. If she does know something she isn't telling, I'm sure I can convince her to tell me what it is—and gently, without frightening her."

"That's something, at least," said Addie.

"You will do as I say now, won't you, Addie? No Ouija boards."

"Well," said Addie, "I suppose you know what you're doing." It was not a reply which eased Harrison's mind.

"Addie. . ." But she was gone.

Chapter Sixteen

Driving home, Harrison had to turn on his windshield wipers. Then he had to turn them on to high speed. "Damn!" he said peevishly.

"Damn!" he said again, as he pulled into the driveway. The house was dark. Matt must be out somewhere—which meant in all probability he would have to fix his own dinner. He fumbled irritably with the light switch as he walked in the door. Nothing happened.

Matt appeared in the hallway, candles in hand. "The lights went off twenty minutes ago," he said. "Looks as though they're out all over town. It's going to be a night of it."

"No electricity," growled Harrison. "If that just doesn't top everything. Seances and dark and stormy nights."

"What?"

Harrison wondered briefly if the lights at Mrs. Otto's school had gone out too.

All that evening he paced about peevishly. He

even snapped at Matt when the older man asked him if anything was wrong. Addie wouldn't . . . and surely not tonight. . .? And what if she did? he asked himself angrily. A child's game, that was all. Nothing whatever to worry about.

"Another Ouija board session?" asked Gwyneth. "But how? Mrs. Otto took away the board."

"I can get it back," said Addie. "Before dinner. I know right where she would put it. It's no problem getting it back."

"But why?" asked Phyllis. "Why, Addie? The Ouija board told us who the murderer is. And it was right. Mr. Linn is as good as arrested. There isn't any question at all, is there?"

"Maybe not," said Addie, "but I'm not so sure. Even Ouija boards make mistakes sometimes. It might know something more now that it's had time to think about it. And besides, we were the ones who told on Mr. Linn. Just supposing he's *not* guilty. We'd have helped send an innocent man to his death."

"You always have to be so dramatic," sniffed Gwyneth. "Well, okay, but I bet you anything— I'll bet you your gold ring against my jade turtle that the Ouija board still says it's Mr. Linn."

"I'd never bet my gold ring. Possibly my fur muff."

"That ratty thing?"

"It's real sable."

"Well, all right. When shall we do it?"

"Up in our room after dinner."

"I don't want to," said Phyllis.

"It can't be what I'm thinking," muttered Harrison later that evening.

"What can't be? Oh, that case again." Matthew got up from the fire, where he had just thrown on another log. "Between you and this storm and the dark . . ." he shook his head. "You're about to drive me crazy, sittin' over there talking to yourself. You always mutter like this when you have a new theory. What is it?"

"I'm thinking about the way I found out about the existence of that diary. . ."

"What are you talking about? Do you think you know who the killer is?"

"It can't be who I'm thinking. It was just a silly idea."

"Why don't you tell me what it is? Maybe it's not so silly."

"No. It's ridiculous. You'd just tell me it was ridiculous—and I don't need you to tell me that. Besides . . . oh, never mind. This case is getting to me, that's all."

But he couldn't shut out the image that had appeared in his mind earlier, and recurred several times since. Harrison looked into the fire. There were some things he couldn't share with Matt, or with Jeff Willes, or with anyone. Things he couldn't say. Matt would think he'd lost his mind. Anyone would . . . except . . . except possibly Addie. Addie might understand, thought

Harrison. Perhaps Addie, even now, was thinking the same things. . . .

He looked again into the fire, and saw an image of a taunting cat and a helpless, desperate mouse. Blackmail, yes, money, yes . . . but more. Lucie Jackson had *enjoyed* her blackmail, enjoyed taunting her victim. Matthew's cat had food of its own. It did not need to catch a mouse.

And Paul . . . Paul was no mouse. He was not desperate. His sense of humor, his core of strength, saved him from it. Lucie Jackson could not have played with him . . . the way she played with . . . someone.

Someone who had a secret. A secret Lucie Jackson knew about. Someone, who finally, could not endure her blackmail, her threats, her taunts. Someone who, finally, had killed her.

But who? Beatrice? Alex? Mrs. Otto? Sarah? Someone else? Someone, thought Harrison, essentially weak. Like the mouse. But no one at Mrs. Otto's school seemed, really, that weak. And yet, people were not always what they seemed. He had thought Beatrice Withers weak and silly, but she had revealed a side of herself in Paul Linn's room that was, as Addie said, "frightening." No, thought Harrison, people were not always what they seemed.

Chapter Seventeen

"Addie, do you really think we ought to do this?" Gwyneth puckered her forehead, looking worried. Outside the window, a cloud-covered half-moon cast strange shadows on the trees. Phyllis looked at the shadows and shivered.

"After I went to all the trouble of sneaking into Mrs. Otto's room and getting back the Ouija board? Of course we have to do it—and right now, before she comes upstairs."

"I don't want to," said Phyllis.

"If you don't," said Addie, "I won't take the board back to Mrs. Otto's room. One of you will have to do it. Or else she'll find it missing, and we'll all get in trouble."

"That's not fair! It was your idea. You did it."

"Makes no difference. Now, are we going to have a Ouija session, or aren't we?"

"I still think you're wasting your time," sulked Gwyneth. "It already said Mr. Linn was guilty. You even agreed. You know you did."

"Yes. But I could have been wrong. Besides, I told you before I didn't think the Ouija was telling us everything."

"Well, maybe you're right. It would be nice if it turned out not to be Mr. Linn," said Gwyneth. "I do like him. And I can't imagine him, really, killing anyone. All right. I'll get a note pad."

"Addie," gasped Phyllis, "in the dark? Can't we wait till the lights come on? Till the storm's over? Tomorrow maybe? It's so scary in the dark."

"That's just the point," said Addie as she lighted a long, tapering candle stolen earlier from the dining room cupboard. "It's better this way." The candle's light cast darting shadows on the walls. (Like fingers, thought Phyllis. Little fingers reaching out to grab you.)

"I'm going to try something different this time," Addie said. "Lucie's ghost knows who killed her. I'm going to try to summon it." Addie shut her eyes. After a moment Phyllis followed suit. At least, thought Phyllis, it was a relief to shut her eyes against those shadows.

"Miss Jackson!" Addie called softly. "Miss Jackson! Are you there? We want to help you. We're trying to help avenge your death. Are you there?"

The silence in the room was thick. Phyllis thought she could hear the flickering of the candle, could hear the beating of her own heart, in that silence. But that was silly. You couldn't hear things like that. It wasn't possible.

"Are you there?" Addie asked again.

Slowly the marker moved toward the 'yes' side of the board.

"Good," said Addie with satisfaction. (How can she be so calm? thought Phyllis.) "Now we're getting somewhere. Now, were we wrong about Mr. Linn having killed you?"

DAMN HIM, the Ouija board spelled tersely.

"What do you suppose *that* means?" questioned Gwyneth. "It just never will give us straight answers."

"You have to be patient, that's all. Miss Jackson? Did Mr. Linn murder you?"

HE COULD HAVE, said the Ouija. It spelled the words out firmly, unhesitatingly.

"But he didn't?" Addie persisted.

NO, the Ouija spelled.

Phyllis gasped. "But . . . why did it say he did the first time?"

WRONG RONG RONG RONG, the Ouija repeated. The marker flew under their hands, circling in a demonic rhythm of its own. RONG RONG

"Stop that!" said Gwyneth, sounding frightened. "If he didn't do it, then who did?"

The Ouija hesitated, then moved slowly in a wide circle. It didn't stop on any letters. It circled again. ("It's watching," whispered Phyllis. "It's watching us.")

"Ssh," said Addie. Slowly, the Ouija board began to spell: P-H-I-L-I-S . . .

Gwyneth gasped. "Wait!" said Addie. "It's not finished."

. . . K-N-O-S.

"Phyllis knows," whispered Gwyneth.

Addie stole a look at Phyllis, who had turned

white. In the pale light of the candle she looked like a ghost herself. "No," she whispered, "no—I don't." She jerked her hands away from the board.

Addie shut her eyes. PHYLLIS SAW, the Ouija board spelled under Addie's hands alone.

"I knew you saw something that night," said Addie triumphantly. "Oh, I didn't know right away, but things began to fall into place. What was it, Phyllis? You can tell us. My uncle will protect you."

"But I didn't, I didn't see anything really."

"Yes you did," said Addie. "Yes you did." But Phyllis only shook her head and rocked back and forth, her eyes squeezed shut. The Ouija began to move, again under Addie's fingers. TELL WHAT YOU KNOW TELL LUCIE.

At that moment, three things happened. Addie was not sure afterwards which came first. There was a crash and someone, Phyllis probably, screamed. The third thing that happened was that the candle went out.

In the total darkness that followed, Addie felt Gwyneth tugging at her arm hysterically. "I told you we shouldn't have done this," Gwyneth whimpered. "We've made Miss Jackson's ghost mad. We've made it mad."

"Oh, for heaven's sake," replied Addie as calmly as she could. "It's nothing like that. Something just happened to make the candle go out. The wind, probably. And Sarah or Mrs. Withers maybe dropped something. Listen, somebody's probably going to be coming in here pretty soon to see if it was us who made that noise. Have you got the board? Put it under the bed. We've got to make sure it's hidden."

She fumbled for the light, but the electricity was still off. An atmosphere in the room she couldn't quite define made her doubly afraid. "Oh," she admitted to herself under her breath, "I do wish now I'd listened to Uncle H. But it's too late now."

There were the sounds of footsteps running, and Addie thought she heard the sound of their door being flung open. It was pitch dark. From far down the hall—or was it downstairs?—Addie heard Beatrice Withers complaining in a high petulant voice and someone, probably Sarah Bow, wailing. There were the sounds of a man's voice—Alex? Paul Linn?—trying to calm them. And somehow, the window was wide open and the wind came howling in.

"Oh, it's the ghost," screamed Gwyneth. "Oh help, it's come to get us. Help! Help!"

"Will you hush?" said Addie. "Come on, we'd better get downstairs." Addie felt Gwyneth on her heels as she found the door and walked, as quickly as she could trust herself, down the dark hall. She heard the door to their room shut behind them. That was odd, Phyllis remembering to shut the door. Addie was glad Phyllis wasn't hysterical too. Gwyneth was as much as she could manage.

"Addie!" It was Harrison, calling from the first floor. "Are you all right?"

So, his was the man's voice she'd heard. "Oh,

I knew you'd come," Addie sighed with relief. "We're all right—we're just now coming down."

They were on the stairs, just starting down, when there was another sound from above them. Gwyneth clutched Addie's arm even tighter. "The ghost," she moaned. "The ghost!" Sarah Bow's shrieks joined Gwyneth's.

"What is going on, Inspector?" came Beatrice's frightened voice. "Why did you come here tonight? Do you know who the murderer is? Do you think the murderer is here . . . now . . . in the dark?"

"You're scaring me, Mrs. Withers," said Gwyneth in a high voice. "You're not to scare us. Mrs. Otto says you're not to scare us."

"I had a feeling something was going to happen tonight," said Harrison grimly. "And it looks as though something has. Where are the others? Alex?"

"I don't know," said Beatrice. "Out in back, probably."

"Paul Linn?"

"We haven't seen him all evening."

"And where is Mrs. Otto?"

"She was going upstairs to bed early," said Beatrice. "Because of her flu."

"I think I'd better go up and make sure she's all right. We still don't know what caused that crash."

"Yes we do, Uncle H," said Addie suddenly from the bottom of the stairs. "There's something here. Some broken glass—and some metal or something. I almost stepped on it."

"Stay there, then," said Harrison. "Don't move. Doesn't anyone have a flashlight? Something besides candles?"

"I think there's one in the kitchen," said Sarah Bow. "I know where it is—I'll get it." She lit a match to guide her way. In a few moments she returned, followed by Alex, who was dripping with rain.

"What's going on?" he asked. "I thought I heard something. What the . . ."

The light shone in the hallway, illuminating a heap of broken glass and crumpled metal.

"Why, it's a mirror," said Sarah. "The one that used to hang in the hallway on the second floor."

"Someone—someone took it off the wall and hurled it down the stairs," said Harrison.

They all looked silently at the broken mirror. "But why?" whispered Sarah Bow. "Why?"

"I don't know," he replied. "Was anyone standing anywhere near this thing when it fell?" He resisted the impulse to flash the light into each of their faces. The dim light made it hard to distinguish between the shadowy figures.

"Not that I know of," said Beatrice. "Sarah and I were in the drawing room by the fire. We couldn't see the hall from where we were sitting. I thought we were the only ones downstairs."

There was a fumbling at the front door, and Paul Linn burst in. He simply stood and stared at the sight which greeted him: a group of dark figures grotesquely lighted and shadowed by the flashlight, clustered around a broken heap of glass on the floor.

"Will somebody please turn on the lights?" demanded Paul Linn. "What are they out for? What the devil is going on?"

"The lights have been out all evening," said Beatrice. "Where have you been?" Paul didn't answer.

"Uncle Harrison," gasped Addie suddenly, "Phyllis is gone! Where is she?"

Gwyneth cried out.

"Wasn't she with you?" Harrison demanded.

"She *was*." Addie fought down panic. "I thought she was with us on the stairs. Oh, no. I knew it—I knew she saw something—she knows who the murderer is—and we were having another Ouija board session—to frighten her into telling us. She did know, she did!"

"Addie, calm down," Harrison said. "Did she tell you?"

"No," Addie replied, her eyes wide and frightened. "But I think she was about to. And then, and then—that's when there was the crash—and the candle wavered—and there was so much commotion—and Gwyneth was screaming—so that we just didn't know. I assumed she was right behind us—but, but, maybe she wasn't!"

"The ghost," whispered Gwyneth. "The ghost was in that room with us, all along."

Addie and Gwyneth looked at each other. Slowly Addie said, "I had the feeling that something was wrong. That something was in that room that shouldn't have been."

"What in the world are you talking about?" demanded Paul Linn. "What's all this about a Ouija board, and Phyllis knowing who did it?"

"We asked the Ouija board, right after Miss Jackson's death, who killed her," Gwyneth babbled. "And it said you did. But then Addie said she thought it might have been wrong, that maybe you didn't do it, that we should ask it again. So that's what we were doing. And Addie was right—it did say you didn't do it. And it said— it said that Phyllis knew who did. Only Phyllis said she didn't know. And then . . ."

Addie broke in. "That's right. Then it said— Phyllis *saw*—which is what I thought all along. That Phyllis did see something that night, only she didn't know what it meant. And it was probably something she wasn't supposed to see, or else she would have admitted it. And I thought if I could make her tell what she saw, I would know what it meant—or I could figure it out. Phyllis isn't too good at figuring things out. But . . . she didn't have a chance to say what she saw, because all of a sudden there was that terrible crash—and the candle went out—and everything was perfect darkness. And we were scared—even I was scared—because we thought, maybe it *was* Miss Jackson's ghost, truly, there in that room with us. And, well, we just came down here . . ."

"The ghost *was* there," said Gwyneth. "The ghost has taken Phyllis. It has!"

"No," said Harrison.

His heart plummeted. All the clues he had ignored. Those small, uncharacteristic gestures of nervousness. All those clues . . . because it had seemed so impossible. But people were not always what they seemed to be—hadn't he just told himself that? Someone like Paul, who seemed weak, could be strong inside. And someone who seemed strong could really be weak, and afraid. And desperate enough to kill.

The person who had known about the diary from the very first. Who had become frightened at the growing realization that things were not going to blow over, that the scandal was not going to die down by itself. Who had seen the chance to frame Paul Linn.

They were all looking at him.

"No," he repeated. "Not a ghost. A person. Standing outside your door. Dropping the mirror to distract you—so Phyllis couldn't tell what it was she saw. The only person who isn't with us in this room right now—the only person who doesn't want Phyllis to reveal what she knows. . ."

Addie gasped. "Mrs. Otto!" she breathed. "Oh, Uncle Harrison, I've just remembered. The something strange I felt in that room. It was a scent. Of something that hadn't been there before. I know now what it was. Liniment. Mrs. Otto has the flu. Nobody else would have liniment on. And then—the window was open, and. . .! Uncle Harrison—what has Mrs. Otto done with Phyllis?!"

"Come on!" Harrison started for the stairs, taking them two at a time.

The window in the girls' room was still open. The curtain was flapping wildly in the wind, looking like a ghost itself. The candle had tipped over, and wax dripped from the desk onto the floor. The Ouija board marker was still there.

"We didn't have the window open," said Gwyneth. "Not like that. But then, somehow, after the crash I think . . . it was open."

"And someone shut the door," said Addie suddenly. "After us. I thought it was Phyllis closing it behind her. But it was Mrs. Otto shutting us out"—she shivered—"and shutting Phyllis in."

Harrison went over to the window. "It's pretty easy to get down," said Addie. "There's the awning and then that tree. We've done it before. Even Phyllis, though she didn't want to and we had to talk her into it. But," said Addie firmly, "she'd never have done it by herself. Never. Mrs. Otto must have made her."

"All right," said Harrison. "She took Phyllis out—somewhere. I've got to find out where." He headed for the stairs. "The rest of you stay here."

"No," said Addie. "We're coming too. It's all my fault."

"You might need our help," said Paul.

"All right," said Harrison. "I haven't got time to argue."

They went out through the kitchen. The wind outside was blowing wildly, whistling through the trees so that Harrison himself was reminded of a ghost's wailing. The sound did nothing to calm Sarah Bow, who accompanied the wind's howling with her own. She would not go back, however, and quieted down somewhat when Harrison threatened savagely to send her back to the dark house.

"Paul," said Harrison, "go to the garage and see if there are any cars missing. Quickly. I'm heading out toward the back."

Harrison stopped in the grass, hearing Paul's footsteps running toward the front of the house, toward the garage. He slowed his breathing, fighting down the adrenalin that raced through his system. He had to think. He couldn't rush around in the night blindly.

The garden path was too dark to follow. Harrison found it difficult to get his bearings amid the swirling wind and rain, and the darkness. He was afraid that even if Mrs. Otto were up ahead of him he would not be able to see her. Not sure what he did expect to see, he strained his eyes and looked ahead of him to . . .

To where a dark object loomed, standing still amid the blowing trees.

The greenhouse.

"That's it!" he whispered. "That's where the diary was. Where—maybe—Mrs. Otto put the diary. The greenhouse. It's got to be." He turned to the others. "Be quiet. Don't make a single sound. Phyllis' life could depend on it."

Their feet rustled in the grass, and for once Harrison was thankful for the wailing wind, which drowned out any sounds they might make. He was thinking back. It seemed like a long time, but he thought, he prayed, that it had truly been only a few minutes since that crash. If he were only right . . . and if he were only in time.

The greenhouse stood before him, closer now, a dark shadow surrounded by trees. The branches of some of the trees brushed against its walls and roof with harsh, rasping sounds. Harrison strained as he approached to hear any other sounds, beyond the trees and wind.

He did. He heard . . . could it be? A high-pitched sound, just audible over the wind's whistling. Singing? It was. But unlike any singing he had ever heard before on earth. That is how it is to be mad, he thought. To make a sound like that.

Addie clutched at him, but Harrison pushed her away. "Stay back, Addie," he whispered. "If you never listen to me again in your life, listen now. Don't go in there."

When he first entered the door, which was open and swinging wildly, he could not see anything. He followed the direction of the singing:

> Yet may you spy the fawn at play,
> The hare upon the green;
> But the sweet face of Lucy Gray
> Will never more be seen.

And then there was laughter. And then the song began again.

It was totally dark. Some instinct told Harrison not to turn on the flashlight which he clutched, but to trust his other senses. He sensed, rather than saw, the outline of a tall figure. Mrs. Otto. He could hear no sounds from Phyllis.

"So it's you, Inspector," came the voice, breaking off its singing. It was Mrs. Otto's voice, all right, but how it had changed! A travesty of that calm superior voice he knew. All the humanness had gone out of it.

"I suppose you don't care to hear me sing. You want to hear my secret, don't you? Everyone wants to hear my secret. Everyone wants to know secrets that they have no right to." Her voice rose hysterically. "But you can't, you know. No, you can't. You're too late. Phyllis won't tell. Phyllis can't tell."

Harrison's heart plunged. So he had been too late. She had already . . .

"No, Phyllis won't tell. Phyllis disobeyed once, but she will be punished. She will never do it again. Phyllis is an obedient child. She will never tell things which she has been forbidden . . . forbidden . . . to tell. Will you, Phyllis? Never ever."

There was a sound, a small animal whimper, and a movement. There was time. With his pulse pounding madly, Harrison flipped on his flashlight, and shone it straight at the dark figure's head.

Mrs. Otto was holding Phyllis against her, a rope held around Phyllis' neck, loosely, its ends clasped fiercely in Mrs. Otto's one hand. With the other hand she held Phyllis tight against her.

When the light flashed at her, Mrs. Otto screamed, a terrible scream, and tightened the rope around Phyllis' neck. . . .

What happened then happened so quickly that no one had time to think.

Paul Linn burst in through the back door of the greenhouse. As Mrs. Otto turned, startled, he put his hands between the rope and Phyllis' neck. He jerked, and with a cry Mrs. Otto let go of the rope as it wrenched through her fingers and burned them.

Harrison dropped the flashlight, and grabbed Mrs. Otto's arms.

But there was no struggle. Mrs. Otto dropped to the floor, sank against the wall, a dazed expression on her face. She went limp, closed her eyes. Harrison took the rope which Paul still held in his hand, and tied it around Mrs. Otto's wrists. She did not protest. "I'm so tired," she told Harrison, and then did not utter another word.

Addie and Gwyneth crept into the greenhouse. Beatrice and Sarah Bow followed. It suddenly seemed very quiet there, and the wind very far away. All eyes turned toward the small white figure huddled in the corner.

Harrison turned the light more fully on Phyllis. She looked up and smiled, but not at Harrison.

"Oh, Mr. Linn," said Phyllis, "I always knew you were a hero."

Chapter Eighteen

Addie was frankly jealous. Phyllis the center of attention—Phyllis being given mugs of coffee with real cream in it (while she, Addie, got only chocolate), not to mention all sorts of other special things—Phyllis being fussed over—Phyllis, who had escaped death by inches—Phyllis, who had practically been *murdered*!

It was the next morning. They were all in the drawing room which seemed somehow, with Mrs. Otto gone, lighter and brighter. Phyllis was seated at one end of the couch in front of the fire, a blanket around her, sipping coffee. "As though she were sick," sniffed Gwyneth. "She's not one bit hurt."

Paul Linn had brought his bottle of brandy out into the open and was giving it much attention.

"I still don't understand," said Phyllis, looking up. "I really *didn't* see anything important the night of the murder. I was up when I wasn't supposed to be. I woke up and couldn't get back to sleep, and then I remembered Sarah Bow had made that new cake. . . ."

"No wonder you didn't tell," put in Gwyneth. "Not only up when you weren't supposed to be, but stealing cake too!"

". . . and I went downstairs. But when I got to the bottom of the stairs, I saw Mrs. Otto—so I quick went back up again. She didn't see me. But she wasn't doing anything. Just standing and looking into the fire. That's all. That's all there was to it."

"But there was no fire that night," reminded Harrison. "It had gone out hours before. Beatrice Withers mentioned that specifically. The fire you saw was Mrs. Otto burning some newspaper clippings that Lucie had in her room and had been using to blackmail her. She almost burned Lucie's diary too—but changed her mind at the last minute. It probably wouldn't have burned properly with that leather cover anyway, but also Mrs. Otto hadn't realized till she looked through it that Lucie was blackmailing Paul too. It gave her the vague idea of framing him later if she needed to."

"I did see something in her hand," said Phyllis. "But I didn't know what it was. She needn't have tried to kill me. I didn't see anything that would have proved her guilty."

"But she didn't know that," said Harrison. "When she listened outside your door last night to the Ouija board session, all she knew was that you were afraid of *something*. She didn't realize that you were simply afraid of confessing that you'd disobeyed. She thought you really did see her kill Lucie, and that you must not be allowed to tell what you saw."

They were all silent a moment. Addie felt a shiver go through her at the thought of what might have happened. Phyllis, however, was calm. She sipped her coffee placidly and nestled herself more snugly under the blanket.

"But why?" asked Gwyneth after a minute. "Why did Mrs. Otto do it? No one's told us anything."

Harrison thought back to the previous night and shuddered. Mrs. Otto had literally come apart under questioning. She had talked, rambled, for what seemed like hours, revealing a story that was fantastic.

He took a deep breath, and began: "Apparently when Mrs. Otto was young, just in her twenties and still living with her parents—her father became drunk one New Year's Eve and brutally killed a woman he'd picked up in a bar. He was convicted of murder and executed.

"If you remember, Lucie came home New Year's Eve with the remark about being afraid of 'drunkards and murderers.' It wasn't just an off-hand remark, as Beatrice thought, but a deliberate twist-of-the-knife, meant to remind Mrs. Otto that she knew her secret.

"Anyway, after the trial, Lenore—or rather Lorraine, as she was known then—couldn't bear the shocked looks and whispers of the townspeople. She even began to be haunted that (as some of the whispers suggested) the insanity of her father might be in her as well. So she ran away to another town, far away, changed her name and identity and became Mrs. Lenore Otto, young widow. After a few years she moved here and bought the school."

Harrison continued. "It seems as though she built that rigid, awe-inspiring reputation for herself in order to blot out any qualities in her or in anything surrounding her that reminded her of her father. A proper, prestigious girls' school was perfect. She instilled values of rigid morality in her students and stressed discipline and etiquette beyond anything else. She hated anything to do with liquor, or with men."

"But," puzzled Phyllis, "you mean the way she pretended to be wasn't really the way she was?"

"Ah," said Harrison, "now we come to the reason, the real reason, why she killed Lucie Jackson. I think Mrs. Otto, up until the time Lucie discovered her secret, had almost blotted the past out of her mind. She had almost convinced herself that the image she had built for herself was really true."

"But Lucie," said Paul, "with her well-known flair for twisting the knife just where people didn't want it twisted, brought all of Mrs. Otto's past back to her."

"That's right."

"How did she find out, anyway?"

"Oh, quite by accident, really. She happened across an old newspaper that carried the story of the father's trial. There was a picture of Lenore at the courthouse—even though the name was different, Lucie thought the woman looked familiar and did some checking up. It wasn't too difficult, once she knew what she was looking for."

"And you're right, Paul," Harrison said approvingly. "That's when Lucie's 'play' began. She taunted Mrs. Otto maliciously, hinted at blackmail, and in general enjoyed herself thoroughly—not realizing, or perhaps not caring, how much she was destroying Mrs. Otto."

"You know," said Addie, "that's why Mrs. Withers hated her. Not just because she was jealous. Mrs. Withers knew Miss Jackson was mean—really mean, not just selfish and thoughtless. Mrs. Withers knows things sometimes."

"Well," Harrison continued, "Mrs. Otto's world crumbled. I think at that point she really did begin to go mad. Would Lucie really destroy her by giving away her secret? She couldn't take that chance. Yet, if she killed Lucie, there would be a scandal of another sort, and that would damage, perhaps even ruin, the school. That idea was unthinkable to Mrs. Otto, because she had come to love the school's reputation almost as much as her own. So she waited, and agonized."

"If we'd known her better," said Paul, "we might have realized something was wrong. We could have helped. Most people wouldn't have cared at all what her father was. But she was so stand-offish and cold."

"I feel sorry for her," said Phyllis.

"Phyllis! She almost killed you," said Gwyneth.

"I don't care," said Phyllis. "I do feel sorry for her."

"Then what happened?" said Addie.

"Then," said Harrison, "came New Year's Eve. With Lucie's well-known flair for the dramatic she chose this time to twist the knife a little deeper. How cruel she was! She didn't demand more money, didn't do anything at all, except to make her one coy remark about 'drunkards and murderers.' Beatrice paid no attention, of course, to this remark—'just more of Lucie's theatrics'—but Mrs. Otto knew then beyond any doubt that she could never trust Lucie to keep her secret. More importantly, she was enraged to madness that Lucie would treat her private tragedy so lightly, as if she found it amusing.

"So, after Beatrice had gone to bed and before Paul had a chance to come home, she slipped upstairs and strangled Lucie while she slept.

"She knew that only the most impossible stroke of luck would make the police think Lucie's death an accident, but maybe . . . the marks on the neck were very faint, she could mention a history of heart trouble, the police force is small and . . . ahem . . . 'not too efficient' (her words). It was worth a try.

"I think she really did feel," said Harrison,

"that her school's reputation was invulnerable. At first. But when an irate mother called threatening to take her daughter away if the murderer wasn't found, she realized that what she was hoping for was impossible. There was no way to prevent a scandal now that talk had already begun. All she could do was hope that no one would suspect her, and maybe, when it was all over, she could go away and start over. She had done that once already, after all.

"It was then that she decided to plant the diary, in a place she was fairly sure it would eventually be found by someone—and then casually mentioned its existence to me in your hearing, Paul."

"Boy, I sure fell into that," said Paul Linn, shaking his head. "Say, Inspector, that reminds me. That night—when I was in Sarah's room looking for the diary—what was all that about Alex being suspicious? His army pin, and the funny way Sarah Bow was acting? What did that have to do with?"

"Nothing," replied Harrison. "Nothing to do with the case, that is. Sarah finally told me. Everyone has little secrets, I guess. Alex is a kleptomaniac. The two times he spent in jail were for petty theft. He just never could break the habit. He would sneak into the house at night occasionally and take things. Never anything big—a cup, a box of candy. Sarah found him out when she began cleaning his room and finding things that shouldn't be there. He confessed to her, and after that things went along smoothly. She kept his secret: he stole things and she put them back. And not a word was said. But she knew if Mrs. Otto ever found out, that would be the end of Alex's job there. That's why she lied."

"That was silly," said Addie. "She could have gotten him arrested for murder. If *we* hadn't been observant and seen that it was really Mr. Linn in her room."

"Yes, and almost got *me* arrested for murder," reminded Paul.

"Well, you did act awfully suspicious," Addie pointed out. "Everyone certainly thought it was you. Right up till the very end."

"That's right," remembered Gwyneth. "Where were you last night, all the time the lights were out? You didn't even know they were out. You didn't come in until after the mirror had crashed. And you were soaking wet from the rain," Gwyneth finished disapprovingly. "Absolutely soaking."

"Oh that," said Paul with discomfort.

"Yes, where were you?" asked Addie. "The lights were off practically all over town. And you didn't even know it. Hmmm," said Addie.

"Now wait a minute," said Paul. "Don't start jumping to conclusions. I thought I was cleared of all suspicion. The fact is," said Paul, "during the time Phyllis was being kidnapped, *I* was being jilted. Much worse experience."

"You don't mean," gasped Phyllis, "that Melissa Willoughby broke your engagement?"

"I do mean it," said Paul. "You know"—he blew a thoughtful smoke ring into the air—"it's not even so much the jilting I mind. It's the way she went about it. The timing. The manner. The ungraciousness of it all." Paul turned to Phyllis confidingly. "She was very ungracious about it. Very.

"I wouldn't have minded that she decided to end it just as I was driving her home," he continued. "Nor that she spitefully decided to take back the sportscar she'd given me though she *had* given it to me—it certainly was not a loan or anything like that. What I did mind was the fact that she did both of those things at the same time. She threw me out of the car and sped off, leaving me out on a deserted country road, in the rain, in the dark—and five miles from home."

"Poor Mr. Linn!" said Phyllis.

"Thank you, my dear."

"And now," said Addie to change the subject —Phyllis was beginning to make sheep eyes at Mr. Linn and they'd had enough of *that* with Mrs. Withers—"what do you suppose will happen? To all the teachers, you know. And the school."

Paul Linn took a generous sip of brandy. "Well," he began. . . .

"Couldn't *you* stay on, Mr. Linn?" asked Phyllis wistfully. "You could buy the school—change its name. Couldn't you?"

"Oh no, my dear," said Paul Linn. "I can't even stand the thought of spending another night in this place. No, I think it's time for me to move on. Particularly now," and he paused, "since I am, er, unengaged. And temporarily without funds.

"Do you know," he asked, turning to Harrison, "of any place where there is an abundance of rich widows? Australia, perhaps? I always thought I would like to visit Australia. I think that's the thing to do now. Find a nice rich widow. I think," he said, "a widow would be a definite improvement over my past choices. Someone mellow, and undemanding—and generous. Even a little on the middle-aged side would be all right. Do you think Australia? An English accent is a nice touch in a woman."

"Cruise ships are good," advised Gwyneth. "My grandmother and her friends go on cruises every year—in packs. They like it because there's dancing every night and the deck stewards dance with them, and even flirt with them a little. It's part of the deck stewards' job, of course, but my grandmother doesn't think about that. You could be a deck steward, Mr. Linn. You'd look very nice in a uniform."

"I would, wouldn't I?" said Paul, considering. "With polished gold buttons down the front. Do cruise ships go to Australia, do you know?"

"Certainly," said Gwyneth. "Cruise ships go everywhere."

"Especially to Australia," said Addie.

"But . . . can't you stay?" asked Phyllis.

"Australia," mused Paul. "It's an idea."

Chapter Nineteen

"Why did you d-d-do that?" sobbed Phyllis, upstairs in the bedroom. She cried into her shepherdess quilt. "Now we'll never see him again. And we'll all be s-s-separated. And have to go h-h-home. And never see each other again."

"The trouble with you, Phyllis," said Addie, "is that you just don't know how to take advantage of a situation. Now, it's obvious that Mr. Linn doesn't want to stay here. And there certainly isn't anyone else you'd want to be head of the school, is there?"

Phyllis shook her head.

"Not that anybody's mother is going to let her come back to this school, anyway, even if there was a school to come back to. My mother's flying down on the next plane to take me away."

"Mine too," said Gwyneth.

Phyllis nodded, tearfully.

"So," said Addie, pausing for dramatic effect, "you can see how ideal the situation is."

Phyllis stared.

"Pay no attention to her, Phyllis," said Gwyneth. "She's just trying to be Miss Know-

Everything again. Just ignore her."

"All right," said Addie. "If you don't want to know, it's fine with me." She began to hum.

Phyllis looked at Gwyneth. Then she looked at Addie. "But . . . I do want to know."

Gwyneth stamped her foot. "So just tell us and get it over with," said Gwyneth.

"Well," said Addie, "all you have to do is put it together. One, Mr. Linn wants to go to Australia. Two, we have all three, especially Phyllis, had a terrible traumatic experience from which we might never recover. Three, Gwyneth's always bragging about how she can get her grandmother to give her anything she wants."

"So I can," snapped Gwyneth.

"Well, here's your chance to prove it," said Addie. She paused once more, dramatically. "Suppose what you wanted more than anything else was a boat trip to Australia. To help you get over your terrible shock. And suppose you couldn't bear to be separated from your very best friends in the whole world. Just suppose that."

"A trip would be educational," said Phyllis. She had stopped crying. "So we could miss school and it wouldn't matter."

"How can we even think about school, after what's happened? It's too much to expect of us," said Addie.

"It could work," admitted Gwyneth. "It really could. My grandmother's coming down with my mother to get me. She's that worried."

"We could help Mr. Linn find a rich lady to marry," said Phyllis.

"Not my grandmother," said Gwyneth. "She's too homely. But someone."

"A beautiful lady with emerald eyes," said Phyllis.

"Amethyst," corrected Addie. "Amethyst eyes are more romantic. And a carved ivory ring on one slender hand."

"And of course an English accent. He requested that specifically." Phyllis smiled.

Harrison and Paul Linn sat contentedly in front of the fire, sharing the very last of the brandy bottle.

"I wonder what's going to happen to old Beatrice now," mused Paul. "And the others. Sarah and Alex."

"Oh, so you didn't know about Sarah and Alex. They're getting married."

"Married!"

"Yes. I think they can find a new job quite easily as a couple. It should work out just fine. Sarah can watch over Alex the way she always has—put back the things he takes. She's still hoping to reform him. Maybe she will, eventually. I told her I wouldn't give him away. She was worried I was going to arrest him.

"As for Beatrice Withers, I just don't know. "I suppose even though she hates teaching, she'll probably look for another teaching job."

"And another man. I always did wonder if

there really was ever a Mr. Withers, or if she just made him up. Well, I hope for her sake she does find a husband," said Paul charitably. "The old buzzard."

Harrison sat back further in his chair and gazed into the fire. He felt quite pleased with himself, now that everything was over. "Well," he sighed with contentment, "at least there's one thing off my mind. By tomorrow, our three young sleuths will all be back with their parents, where they belong. I never could understand why Sally wanted to ship Addie practically across the country to a private school. I'm sure there's some perfectly normal, average junior high she can go to. Play hopscotch, you know, things like that. Pick apples on the way home," he mused nostalgically.

Paul put down his brandy glass. "In downtown Chicago?"

Harrison looked into the fire and smiled. "It'll be good for Addie," he said, "to do all those regular kid things. Play tetherball. Ride a bicycle. I could even buy her the bicycle."

Gwyneth tried on the blue dress with ruffles down the front, the one that her grandmother said made her look like "a little angel." She studied her reflection in the mirror.

Phyllis nodded. "Yes," she said. "That's good."

"It'll take some doing," said Gwyneth. "I'm not saying it won't." She tied a matching blue ribbon into her hair.

"Addie," asked Phyllis, "are you sure we can find a beautiful lady with amethyst eyes in Australia?"

Addie sat looking out the window at the now-clear sky, at the garden, and the greenhouse roof beyond. She turned around, looked at them both, and smiled.

"I'm positive," said Addie.

Peggy McKier

110038